£2·99
9B

Carry On England

The wickedly funny story that
starts where the film ends

Norman Giller

Chameleon

For Lisa
My precious, precocious princess

First published in Great Britain in 1996 by
Chameleon Books
106 Great Russell Street
London WC1B 3LJ

CIP data for this title is available
from the British Library

ISBN 0 233 99028 3

Typeset by Falcon Oast Graphic Art

Printed in Great Britain by WBC, Bridgend

Author's Acknowledgements

This book could not have been written without the original foundation work of *Carry On* film creators Peter Rogers and Gerald Thomas. I have simply carried on where they left off, but I would not even have managed the first step without their marathon screen productions to inspire me. I am also indebted to the *Carry On* team of actors, who brought their characters to life on screen and turned the film series into a national institution. I acknowledge, too, the lovingly crafted screenplays of the writers, in particular Talbot Rothwell and Norman Hudis. The original screenplay for *Carry On England* was written by Jack Seddon and David Pursall. On behalf of the Publishers, I thank the Rank Organisation for allowing us to step into the *Carry On* territory that has always been exclusive to the silver screen, and for their permission to use still photographs from the original film version of *Carry On England*.

My thanks also to VCI Chief Executive Steve Ayres for letting me off the leash, and to Tim Forrester, Tom Rosenthal and John Cleary at Chameleon for their encouragement; also to my House Editor Stephanie Goodwin and to Richard Percy, who first had the brainwave to turn the *Carry On* films into books. Most of all, thanks to Eileenalanna, Lisa and Michael for being there. The characters and events depicted on the following pages are entirely fictitious, and anybody who wishes to argue otherwise will be laughed out of court. *Carry On Laughing...*

Introduction

This book carries on where the film *Carry On England**
left off. The story so far:

Shell-shocked Captain S Melly (Kenneth Connor) has
been made commanding officer of an experimental
mixed anti-aircraft battery that combines the grit of the
gunners in the artillery with the guile of the girls in the
ATS. Brigadier General Horace Arkwright (Peter Jones)
and Major Cardew Carstairs (Peter Butterworth) have
set up the top-secret unit on the express instructions of
Prime Minister Winston Churchill, who believes that a
mingling of the sexes could do wonders for the morale
of the troops.

It certainly does wonders for the spirit of the barracks
in which Sergeants Able (Patrick Mower) and Willing
(Judy Geeson) lead the way in showing that it is better

---

*The classic comedy film *Carry On England* is available in the *Carry
On* series on Cinema Club videos, distributed by VCI, price £4.99.

to make love than war. Corporal Jack Ready (Jack Douglas) and dispatch rider Johnny Biker (Johnny Briggs), along with Gunner Shorthouse (Melvyn Hayes) and Private Easy (Diane Langton), give enthusiastic support as the unit is whipped into shape by bullying, bellowing Sergeant-Major Bloomer (Windsor Davies), who is himself drawn into the kissing game by man-mad Private Jennifer Ffuchs-Shafte (Joan Sims).

Remarkably and against all odds and expectations, they become heroes and heroines when shooting down a black cloud of German bombers heading across the South Coast on the way to drop their deadly cargo on London.

The unit has now been strengthened, or more probably weakened, by the arrival of desert war veterans Sergeant Sydney Roper (Sidney James), Private Bernie Biddle (Bernard Bresslaw) and a lance-corporal passing himself off as Major Francis Bigger (Frankie Howerd). Also new on duty are medical orderlies James Kilmore (a Jim Dale lookalike) and Kenneth Tinkle (Kenneth Williams), and an extremely forward, in the physical sense, Cockney auxiliary nurse called Sheila Blige (bearing an uncanny resemblance to Barbara Windsor).

They have just arrived at their cosy new posting somewhere in the south of England when Winston Churchill assigns a new and dangerous top-secret mission for just a handful of them: the chosen few who will be owed so much by so many.

Now *Carry On reading...*

Personal memo
from the Prime Minister
10 Downing Street
To: Field Marshal Montgomery
Wednesday, 5 April 1944

Dear Bernie,

I hope this letter finds you in fine fettle, and looking forward to the final big push against the Boche. Well, my old china, the time has now come to launch Operation Ratcatcher which we discussed last month.

I leave it to you to select a 12-strong squad to report to my personal adjutant at my south coast headquarters this coming Monday at 900 hrs. They do not necessarily have to be élite troops, but they do need to be expendable.

Destroy this memo after reading it. I shall keep a copy. You never know, it may one day help my family win a lottery.

Chin up, cheers

Winston S. Churchill

1

SERGEANT-MAJOR Bloomer gnashed his teeth as he peered from beneath the peak of his cap at the soldiers, twenty-seven men and twenty-seven women, loosely paraded in front of him on the barracks square. 'Never in all my born days 'ave I seen such a shower,' he bellowed, disturbing the afternoon nap of Captain Melly, three hundred yards away in the commanding officer's hut. 'Just 'ow we is winning the war with you lot on our side is beyond the apprehension of a mere mortal like what I am.'

The Sergeant-Major paused and smouldered as he saw a hand rise in the front ranks. He bristled as he noticed that it was attached to the arm of Medical Orderly and Temporary Gunner Tinkle, who had recently arrived at the unit through a transfer mix-up and who had quickly proved himself too much of a clever Dick for Bloomer's taste. 'What is it, Temporary Gunner Tinkle?' he asked, dropping each word like a hand-grenade.

'I just think, Sergeant-Major,' Tinkle said in his peculiar nasal whine, 'that when you said "apprehension" you actually meant comprehension, if you comprehend.'

The regulars in the unit collectively sucked in their

7

breath and silently counted to ten, in anticipation of an explosion from the Sergeant-Major. They were not disappointed. Bloomer quick-marched from the centre of the parade and came to a dramatic halt directly in front of Tinkle, his shining black army boots crashing with a "bang-bang" effect on the ground in a regulation coming to attention. He bent forward until his face was just inches from Tinkle's. 'When I need lessons in how to speak proper from little weasels like what you are, I will ask,' he roared. 'Until then keep your mouth shut and your ears open, because you might learn something about how to be a proper soldier. Is that com-pre-hen-ded?'

Tinkle nodded. 'Anything you say,' he mumbled.

'Anything you say, what?' shouted Bloomer.

'Anything you say to me.'

'Sir!' boomed the Sergeant-Major, his eyes bulging and his cheeks turning from crimson to a shade closer to purple. 'Anything you say to me, *Sir*!'

Tinkle was saved from any further assault on his eardrums by the arrival of a sleepy-eyed Captain Melly, known throughout the unit as 'Smelly' because of his initial 'S' for Samuel.

Bloomer quick-marched back to his central place in front of the parade and his precision salute was returned with little more than a half-hearted wave by Melly, who had just about had his fill of this command. All he wanted was for this bloody war to be over so that he could return to his farm down in Somerset and concentrate on his cattle raising, bee-keeping and home-brewing. Beef, bees and beer, not necessarily in that order.

8

'I've just received word that the B-G is coming here in an hour,' Melly said. 'Wants to address the men.'

There was a forced cough from Sergeant Iris Willing in the front ranks, and Melly corrected himself.

'Men *and* women,' he said. 'Apparently he's got orders that have come down to him from the PM, through Monty and on down through the chain of command until it was dumped on the Brigadier-General. We will be as low as they can get.'

Bloomer's carefully groomed military moustache twitched with excitement. He had been aching for involvement in the war that gave him something more of a challenge than trying to stop the randy gunners and the more than willing ATS girls going at each other like rabbits.

'Any hint of what the horders is, Sir?' he asked.

'All I know is that the B-G will be asking for volunteers,' Melly said in a matter-of-fact way. 'Said something about a dangerous mission.'

There was a sharp intake of breath among the ranks that sounded like a balloon being punctured. They had overheard two words that they had spent great energy avoiding during the run of the war, *volunteer* and *dangerous*.

'Dismiss the men... and women,' said Melly. 'We shall want them on parade again for the B-G in an hour.'

'P-a-r-a-d-e,' bellowed Bloomer, making the captain wince, 'd-i-s-m-i-s-s-e-d.'

As the company came to attention, wheeled right and then broke up in an untidy tangle, the Sergeant-Major shouted: 'You are all to report back here to the parade

9

ground in one hour. You will be haddressed by the Brigadier-General.'

'Undressed more like it,' said Nurse Sheila Blige. 'That dirty old blighter is always undressing us girls with his eyes.'

'You'd much rather us do it with our 'ands, eh love,' said Sergeant Sydney Roper, who during his short time with the unit had already earned the nickname among the ATS girls of 'Roper the Groper'.

Bloomer's eyes danced from side to side under the peak of his cap as he watched the soldiers and, as he called them, the soldieresses, going into urgent huddles, obviously discussing what they had overheard the Captain telling him.

His steely stare came to a halt on a sight he could not believe. There, right in the middle of the parade ground, that man Tinkle had his arms locked in an unhealthy embrace around the backside of another 'dodgy' medical orderly, Kilmore, who was bending over in front of him. If it had been a heterosexual act, Bloomer just might have turned a blind eye to it because that sort of thing was rife in this loosely run camp that, to his mind, was a disgrace to the British Army. But to have two pansies performing in public was too much for him to bear.

He quick-marched the fifty yards to where the gross indecency was taking place. 'Oi, you,' he yelled, 'just what d'you think you're up to? In his Majesty's uniform, too. If you're up to what I think you're up to, you're up to your necks in it.'

Tinkle, who was actually pulling Kilmore by the hips,

looked at the approaching thundercloud that was the Sergeant-Major, let go of his fellow orderly and quickly stood to attention. As he was released, Kilmore suddenly pitched slowly forwards and silently disappeared from sight.

'What is going on, you disgusting pair?' roared Bloomer, who was not nicknamed Tiger for nothing. 'You can't do that sort of thing here. In fact you can't do that sort of thing anywhere, you perverted people, you.'

'It's Corporal Kilmore, Sir,' blurted Tinkle. 'He's gone down a hole.'

'Don't you talk dirty to me, you little toerag,' fumed Bloomer. 'The hole you talk of is meant for only one thing and that is for making deposits. We don't stand for nancy boys in the British Harmy.'

'I don't know what you're twittering on about, Sir,' said Tinkle. 'All I'm telling you is that Corporal Kilmore has fallen down a bloody big hole. Look for yourself.'

The Sergeant-Major's boggling stare followed Tinkle's pointing finger, and he saw that Kilmore was indeed down a bloody big hole.

'Get out of there at once, you silly soldier,' he shouted. 'How did you get down there?'

'The ground just gave way when you shouted your dismissal order, Sir,' said Kilmore, getting out with the help of a tug from Tinkle. 'It must be an old bomb crater that's opened up.'

'Well now you two boys can spend the next hour filling the 'ole in,' said Bloomer. 'I want that 'ole elaminated before the Brigadier-General arrives. This is where we will put the podium from which he will haddress the troops what is gathered before him.'

Tinkle raised an arm. 'I think, Sergeant-Major,' he said, 'that when you said "elaminated" what you actually meant was eliminated.'

If looks could kill, Tinkle would have found his final burying place there and then. 'One of these days, Temporary Gunner Tinkle,' he said with all the menace he could muster, 'I will fill *you* in.'

He marched closer to give him another ear bashing, not realising that the edge of the crater was widening by the second. Bloomer's highly polished boots slid from under him, and he went head first into the hole from which Kilmore had just been pulled.

There was a muffled oath. 'All right, you soldiers,' came a subdued voice from the hole, 'at the count of three, p-u-l-l.'

Out of his view, Kilmore and Tinkle were hugging each other again. They were not consenting adults, but helpless with suppressed laughter.

Brigadier-General Horace Arkwright, veteran of a battle too many and a bridge too far, gave a barely discernible shake of the head as he looked down from the podium at the special unit ranged before him. The order had come down the line to find twelve 'expendable' soldiers. Never had he felt so spoilt for choice.

'I have come here today in search of excellence,' he said, lying through poorly fitted false teeth that clattered like Spanish castanets as he spoke. 'I am seeking twelve élite soldiers of either gender to take part

12

in a secret mission that gives the participants a once-in-a-lifetime chance to serve their country. Perhaps even to *save* their country.'

The B-G looked at the intent faces of his audience taking in his every word. His gaze fell upon Nurse Sheila Blige, or more accurately upon her vast frontage and he momentarily lost his concentration as he imagined burying his face in the vast cleavage.

'As you stand there two abreast I am looking for six pairs to give me succour,' he drooled. 'Yes, suckers, your country needs YOU.'

He pointed directly at Nurse Blige. 'Yes, YOU,' he shouted, with dribble running down his chin. 'Stick your chest out with pride for your country, and I say that with great feeling. How about making an old man happy and letting me have a feel, you lovely filly you.'

Captain Melly gently pushed him to one side before the troops noticed that he had gone a little astray with his intended briefing.

'So men... and women,' Melly said, 'you've heard the Brigadier-General's, uh, moving and emotional address and, speaking as your commanding officer, I want to say how deeply proud I am that it is our battery that has been considered worthy of the honour of providing an élite force. It is about time that we became a force to be reckoned with.'

The Brigadier-General had recovered his composure, and he stepped in front of the Captain on the cramped podium. 'What I should add,' he announced, 'is that I am in actual fact looking for only ten volunteers from among you chaps and chappesses. The Captain here, and the Sergeant-Major, will set an example by joining the mission whether they like it or not.'

Bloomer beamed, while the suddenly white-faced Captain Melly could have screamed. All he wanted was his beef, his bees and his beer.

The Sergeant-Major took centre stage on a podium designed for two. 'Now is the time for you to show what you is made of, you lucky lads and lasses,' he bellowed, with such a high decibel count that the B-G covered his ears. 'You have heard the Brigadier-General say that this mission is a once-in-a-lifetime chance to serve your country. Now, as they say, is the time to put hup or shut hup.'

His beetling eyes flicked back and forth across the fifty-four soldiers on parade, split equally between the two sexes. 'Right, all those who is prepared to volunteer take one step forward,' he ordered.

There was a sudden en masse movement as forty-eight of the company took one smart step backwards, leaving new recruits Kilmore, Tinkle, Bigger, Roper, Biddle and Nurse Blige standing on the same spot and exposed as reluctant volunteers.

'Well would you believe it,' said Francis Bigger, king of the con men. 'We've been conned.'

'It's a dead liberty,' said Gunner Bernie Biddle, who was an undertaker's assistant in civvy life and who saw everything relative with death.

'I'm going to be punching a few 'eads in when we're back in the barracks,' said Sergeant Sydney Roper, whose flattened nose was visible proof of his profession as a middleweight boxer.

'Ooh, stop mucking about,' was all that Kenneth Tinkle could manage.

'Oh well, it's got to be a better posting than this,' said James Kilmore, who was ever the optimist.

'Cor, what a bleedin' carry on,' said Sheila Blige.

'Well done and congratulations,' said the Brigadier-General, 'particularly to the wonderul pair there.' He was looking at Nurse Blige again, and beginning to dribble.

'We are still looking for four more volunteers,' said the captain. 'Come on now. Remember Lord Kitchener. Your country needs you.'

To hammer home his point, he jabbed a finger straight ahead of him Kitchener-style just as the B-G turned to tell him to shut up. His finger sunk deep into the Brigadier-General's left eye socket, and he staggered off the podium with his hands to his face.

While the Captain, with expert help from Nurse Blige, attended to the B-G, the Sergeant-Major took over. 'Right,' he roared, 'those who want to join our six brave volunteers here for a mission of a lifetime, take one step forward.'

Forty-eight soldiers smartly took one step back, looking like a well-drilled formation dance team.

Bloomer began to boil. 'I will give you one more chance,' he yelled. 'Volunteers, please take just one step f-o-r-w-a-r-d.'

Again, forty-eight soldiers in six rows of eight took one step back. Those in the back line of the squad now had their backs to the wall of the cookhouse.

'There's only one way to settle this,' said the

Brigadier-General, climbing back on to the podium after reluctantly parting from Nurse Blige. 'We will play the blindman's version of Russian roulette.'

The Sergeant-Major looked at him blankly. 'And pray, Sir, how does we do that?'

'Simple,' said the B-G. 'We blindfold all the men... and women. Then we spin each of them as you would the barrel on a pistol. We paint a red line down the middle of the parade ground, and while they are still giddy tell them to walk forward while the band plays. The four people closest to the line when the music stops will be our volunteers.'

Perhaps the Brigadier-General had tried to cross several bridges too far.

'Apart from the fact that we do not 'ave any blindfolds, red paint nor a Harmy band, Sir, that is a very good hidea,' said the Sergeant-Major, trying hard not to laugh in front of or, much more serious, *at* a superior officer. 'I think that we just possibly need something a little more practical.'

'How about a raffle?' said the Captain, who had now rejoined them on the podium. 'Put all the names in a hat, and the first four drawn out are the volunteers. Or perhaps it would be fairer if it were the last four whose names come out. It would make it more exciting, don't you think?'

'You can't go raffling soldiers,' said the B-G. 'It's not the done thing. This is a man's Army.'

His gaze fell on Nurse Blige again. 'Well, almost.'

The increasingly frustrated Sergeant-Major was about to suggest that he should simply volunteer the four names himself when he noticed out of the corner of his eye a raised hand that, inevitably, belonged to Clever Dick Tinkle.

'You is interrupting what is a very himportant conference, Temporary Gunner Tinkle,' he warned. 'It had better be something worthwhile and not your usual trivial twaddle.'

'I just wanted to suggest, Sir,' he said, 'that you could end this impasse by perhaps offering an incentive.'

'Oh, yes, and what might that be Mr Smarty-Pants?' said the Sergeant-Major. 'Offer them some sweeties, perhaps, or a side of Captain Melly's black market beef?'

Melly blushed and coughed into a fist as the B-G looked daggers at him. 'I thought you only supplied HQ, Smelly,' he said. 'Damned poor show that the lower ranks know about this.'

'Well, Temporary Gunner Tinkle,' continued Bloomer, 'what is your so-clever suggestion?'

'I was thinking of the incentive of honourable discharge from the Army as soon as the mission is over,' he said.

'Honourable discharge?' boomed Bloomer, turning to the Captain and the B-G. 'Have you hever 'eard such a thing? Honourable discharge, I asks you.'

Captain Melly was just about to make it a chorus of derision when he was silenced by the B-G.

'What a bloody spiffingly good idea,' said the Brigadier-General. 'Announce that to the troops this instant, Sergeant-Major. An honorary discharge for the volunteers who survive... who *serve* on this assignment.'

Bloomer faced the remainder of the company, who

were now all backed up against the cookhouse in a straight line so that nobody could be seen volunteering ahead of anybody else. Several had managed to get themselves even further back inside the cookhouse, much to the annoyance of the cook who was trying to prepare that evening's meal. It was called his 'Sausages à la Winston Churchill,' which consisted of two sausages served standing up in mashed potato in the shape of a V-sign.

'What we has decided,' the Sergeant-Major shouted through cupped hands, 'is that the first four of you what gets here to the podium where we are will not only volunteer for the mission... but also be rewarded for your loyalty to King and country with an honourable discharge from His Majesty's Harmy once the hassignment is over.'

The sound of forty-eight soldiers – Gunners and ATS girls – making the fifty-yard dash to the podium suddenly sounded like a herd of charging buffalo. But they were drowned out by the roar of a Norton 350cc motorcycle as Corporal Johnny Biker, a dispatch rider who had joined the unit by accident after getting lost, roared into first place at the podium. Second, sitting in the sidecar filing her nails for future reference, was ATS Private Jennifer Ffuchs-Shafte.

First of the foot soldiers to make it to the podium was the long-legged Corporal Jack Ready, who darted to the front despite the handicap of having Gunner Shorthouse riding on his back like a demented jockey. The ten volunteers had selected themselves.

Sergeant-Major Bloomer had just finished noting

18

down the names when the rest of the field came galloping up to the podium, which gently tilted and then disappeared into a hole that had been covered but not eliminated.

Captain Melly, the Brigadier-General and Bloomer toppled on top of each other into the hole.

'Right, at the count of three somebody up there start to p-u-l-l,' bellowed the Sergeant-Major to what was a suddenly deserted parade ground.

There was not a volunteer in sight.

TOP SECRET
Read and digest
Personal memo
from the Caravan HQ
of Field Marshal Montgomery
To: The Prime Minister
Friday, 7 April 1944

Dear Winnie,

We Opewation Watcatcher

Your orders have been cawwied out. Twelve volunteers, expendable wather than élite, will be weporting to your South Coast HQ on Monday at 900 hours for briefing by your adjutant, Colonel Waymond Wavenscroft.

I hope this make-shift 'volunteer suicide squad' help in the catching of the Wat before the Wat catches you.

Incidentally, I shall be saving a copy of this note for my memoirs. Make sure you destroy it before the Wat gets a peep. Pip, pip old fweind

Bernie Montgomerwy

2

CAPTAIN Melly took down the top-secret orders by telephone himself from a man introducing himself as Winston Churchill's personal aide. The mere mention of Churchill's name made the hair stand up on the back of Melly's neck. 'This,' he thought to himself, 'must be a key assignment if the PM is involved.' The aide told him clearly that the special detachment of volunteers was to report to him at the very hush-hush HQ at Woddington Hall, Woddington, Dorset, at 900 hours on Monday where they would be briefed as to their mission. The codeword Melly had been given was WHALE STATION.

The gatekeeper at Woddington Hall looked at him suspiciously when he whispered 'whale station' to him from the front passenger seat of the army truck being driven by Gunner Biddle. 'What's that you'm be saying?' shouted the gatekeeper, a crotchety old man who would not see seventy again.

'Whale station,' Melly shouted after first of all looking around to make sure nobody else was in earshot.

'Got no whale station, 'ere,' the gatekeeper said in an accent as thick as Dorset cream. 'You'm better off trying Wales.'

'It's our codeword, silly man,' the Captain shouted. 'You've got to let us through. We're already running late.'

Melly would never again detail Gunner Biddle to drive him anywhere. They had driven the hundred and sixty miles to Woddington from their barracks on the Kent coast at an average twenty miles per hour, Biddle insisting that it was the fastest he had been trained to drive in his civvy job as a hearse driver.

The gatekeeper was adamant to the point of bloody-mindedness. 'Oi'm under strict instructions not to allow anybody in or out,' he said. 'So push off and go where the war is. You'm ain't coming in 'ere.'

He checked that the one-bar wooden barrier blocking the drive was secure, and then he stomped off into his small gatekeeper's lodge and loudly slammed the door shut.

It was Sergeant-Major Bloomer, squashed on the front seat between the massive frame of Biddle and the tiny figure of the Captain, who worked out what was going on. 'It's an initiative test,' he said, 'that's what it is. They wants us to prove that we can hovercome hobstacles like what this is. We must show them that we are the élite troops what they are expecting by finding a way past the gatekeeper.'

'What d'you suggest we do, Sergeant-Major?' Melly asked, a past master at delegating duties, decisions and responsibility.

Bloomer studied the twelve-foot high wall surrounding the grounds of Woddington Hall, and took particular note of the barbed wire decorating the top.

'We have no climbing or cutting gear with us, Sir,' the Sergeant-Major said after careful consideration. 'So there is only one thing for it. We must smash our way through the barrier.'

'A corker of an idea, Sergeant-Major,' said Melly. 'Okay Biddle, foot on the accelerator for a change and go full tilt through the barrier. We'll show them just what initiative is all about.'

The Captain looked back over his shoulder. 'Hold tight back there, men,' he shouted to the nine other members of the unit sat huddled together in the back. 'It might get a little bumpy.'

'What about us women?' replied Nurse Blige. 'Ain't we got to 'old on to nuffink?'

Captain Melly had never got used to having men *and* women under his command. '*All* of you hold tight,' he snapped. 'Gunner Biddle is just about to break the barrier.'

'Well it won't be the sound barrier, that's for sure,' said Sergeant Roper. 'I've been in faster bleeding rowing boats.'

Biddle, bubbles of perspiration standing out on his forehead, reversed to the top of the country lane leading to Woddington Hall and revved up the engine. He felt like Malcolm Campbell at the controls of Bluebird. The army truck was going all of twenty-eight miles an hour as it crashed through the barrier, making the gatekeeper jump out of his chair with shock. Within seconds he was on the telephone to the cottage of PC Shufflebottom, the village constable.

'Some maniacs in an army truck 'as broken into the asylum,' he shouted into the receiver. 'Oi thinks we'd better try to keep 'em in.'

And so it was that a sheepish Captain Melly sat in

the Woddington Hall office of Dr Hammerskill explaining to the doctor and PC Shufflebottom how and why his army truck had smashed down the barrier. In the confusion, eight of the maddest people in Dorset had escaped and now Dr Hammerskill, head psychiatrist at the mental home, was seriously considering whether he had found twelve patients to take their place. Since arriving from Switzerland a year earlier, Dr Hammerskill had never quite adjusted to just how many seriously insane people there were in Britain, or even in just this little corner of Dorset. 'I zink zey eat too much roast beef when it is obvious to me zat zer cows are alzo mad,' he had written back to colleagues he had left behind in Zurich to take this post at Woddington Hall.

Shufflebottom, the latest in a long line of Shufflebottoms to serve in the police force, had never known anything like this before and he was sure none of his predecessors on the village beat had either during their law-enforcing duties.

'Now let me get this straight,' he said in a slow-drawl Dorset accent. 'You'm asking the good doctor 'ere and moiself to believe that you'm on a special mission for Winston Churchill, and that you'm all volunteered to come 'ere to Woddingtom 'all?'

Captain Melly nodded. 'That is correct,' he said. 'We are all volunteers.'

'Vell normally people have to have a zertificate to come in here,' said Dr Hammerskill. 'But I zuppose ve could make an exception in your special case. I'm sure I vould have no problem convincing the powers-zat-be in zer Ministry of Health zat ve should issue zertificates

24

at the greatest possible speed.'

He made notes on his pad: "Mass desertion from Army... Soldiers, male and female, seeking asylum... Zey are volunteering to stay with us... Clear case of battle fatigue... Zer captain is completely mad... Zays he is here on ze orders of Churchill... One of ze deserters has a great pair of knockers."

Melly was now wondering if perhaps this was still some sort of initiative test. He leant forward and spoke in a loud whisper. 'If I say whale station to you,' he said, 'would that get us accepted?'

'Uh, yes,' said the doctor, heavily underlining the 'captain is completely mad' line, 'that vould be quite acceptable.'

Melly relaxed in his chair and laughed with relief. 'Wow, you had me going there for a while,' he said. 'Great wheeze to pass this off as a mad house. Sorry we're late, but it's Gunner Biddle's fault. He drives a hearse, y'see. Must congratulate you two on your disguises. And that Austrian accent, Doctor...'

'It is Sviss,' said Dr Hammerskill.

'Really?' said Melly. 'I went to Switzerland on my last holiday before this silly war broke out. Skiing in the Alps. On the French side of Switzerland. Lovely people, the French-Swiss. Not quite so gutteral as you, but it certainly adds to the reality of it all. Very Freudian. And your white coat and everything. Does Winnie wear a disguise, too, when he comes here?'

'Um, not alvays, Captain,' said Dr Hammerskill, silently wondering whether a straitjacket would be needed.

Meantime seven of the escaped patients had been recaptured. They had forced Biddle to drive them away from the mental home in the army truck, and they had gone just ten miles in an hour when they were stopped by military police. They were back in Woddington Hall within ten minutes of being caught.

The military police immediately reported the break in at the mental home by a dozen people posing in army uniform to HQ. It was clear to them that they would need careful screening. An immediate security blanket was thrown on the incident, and two hours later a steaming angry Brigadier-General Arkwright was on the scene.

He was shown into the room where Captain Melly was being questioned.

'All right, gentlemen, I want to talk to him alone,' he told Dr Hammerskill and PC Shufflebottom.

The doctor was concerned. 'I don't zink zat is advisable,' he said. 'I am afraid zis man is showing all the symptoms of advanced schizophrenia and I cannot vouch for your safety.'

'Just get out,' barked the Brigadier-General. 'This is already a big enough farce without you turning it into something from Dr Jekyll and Mr Hyde. Go and shrink your own head.'

He glared at Melly. 'What the hell are you doing breaking into a looney bin?' he asked, his loose false teeth dancing a fandango. 'Most people try to break out of them. If this story becomes public property, we will be a laughing stock.'

Melly knew when his initiative was really being put

to the test. 'Sorry, Sir, but I have to say that you've blown your cover now,' he said. 'Your uniform is a dead giveaway. Hope the enemy are not watching.'

'What on earth are you twittering on about?'

'Your uniform,' Melly said. 'What with us arriving in an army truck and now you in a Brigadier-General's uniform, why everybody for miles around will now know that this is an army establishment.'

'This place,' seethed the B-G through teeth as clenched as he could get them, 'is a registered, bona fide mental institution. A nut house.'

Melly clapped his hands together in appreciation. 'What a great cover,' he said. 'Mind you, I hope the newspapers don't get the wrong idea if they ever spot Winnie checking in here. That would never do. Imagine the headline: 'WINSTON IN MAD HOUSE'. We all know that it's Hitler, not Winnie, who's the nutty one.'

'Shut up and listen, you idiot,' yelled the B-G. 'I'm telling you just this once and just this once only. This is *not* an army establishment. It is *not* Churchill's South Coast HQ. And you are definitely *not* supposed to be here.'

'But I was given express orders to report here at 900 hours,' said a confused Melly. 'Admittedly we got here late, but that was because Biddle thought he was driving a hearse. Winston Churchill's aide specifically told me on the telephone Woddington Hall, Woddington.'

'Roddington Hall, Roddington,' screamed the Brigadier-General. 'The next bloody village.'

With dispatch rider Corporal Johnny Biker at the wheel

27

and slow coach Gunner Biddle relegated to a seat at the back of the army truck, the 'volunteer suicide army' – as Field Marshal Montgomery had dubbed them – set off for Roddington Hall. PC Shufflebottom pointed them in the right direction out of the south end of the neighbouring village of Woddington, and then cycled home for his tea and with unbelievable tales for the rest of the villagers about crazier than usual goings on at the mad house.

Corporal Biker was a faster driver than Biddle. Much faster. He was speeding round the tight country lanes of Dorset as if on his motorcycle, and Captain Melly was the first to throw up the pork and fried egg luncheon they had been given at Woddington Hall.

The Corporal was proud of his reputation for being one of the quickest of all soldiers at the driving wheel or the handlebars, but his sense of direction did not quite match his sense of speed.

It was four hours later and PC Shufflebottom was just starting out on his bicycle on his late-evening beat when he spotted the army truck, still with the Woddington Hall barrier stuck on the front grille, driving into the north end of Woddington village.

Gunner Biddle was restored to the driver's wheel as the constable cycled ahead of the truck, leading them on the four mile route to Roddington Hall. The only slight problem they had this time was when PC Shufflebottom at one stage got too far ahead, and had to wait at crossroads for the funereal-paced Biddle to catch him up.

The constable stopped at the top of the lane leading

down to Roddington Hall. 'This is as far as oi'm allowed to go,' he said. 'You are now about to enter restricted Ministry of Defence land. The 'all will be facing you'm when you go round the next bend a moile down this lane.'

'We've been round the bend enough today to last us a lifetime,' said Sergeant Roper, who was still trying to recover from his unnerving experience at Woddington Hall when one of the inmates had been convinced that he was the Messiah returned to save the world.

Roper had used his ripest East End language when his declared disciple started kissing his feet, and the inmate had now decided that this was the new word of the Lord. When the volunteers left Woddington, staff at the asylum were still trying to persuade the inmate to come down off the roof from where, hands clasped in prayer, he was effing and blinding on his knees towards the heavens.

PC Shufflebottom had just cycled out of sight when the engine of the army truck gave a couple of unforgiving gasps and died. They had managed to run out of petrol.

The mile to the next bend as calculated by PC Shufflebottom turned out to be at least two miles, and when the reluctant volunteers finally reached it on foot – dragging themselves through rain coming down in stair rods – they were just able to make out the shadowy outline of blacked-out Roddington Hall a further mile away. It looked as spooky as a Count Dracula castle.

It was after midnight when they at last made it to the high, forbidding walls of the Hall, and a tired and irritable Captain Melly was just leading a search for the way in when they were all of a sudden silhouetted in a dazzling pool of blinding light thrown out by a powerful searchlight.

'What the fu--!' Roper started to exclaim when a stentorian voice boomed out.

'Halt! Who goes there? Friend or foe?'

'Depends on who's asking,' said a dripping wet Captain Melly in an out of character frivolous manner brought on entirely by fatigue.

This was not within the compass of replies included in the sentry guidebook, and the suggested response if there was any doubt was: SHOOT FIRST, ASK QUESTIONS LATER.

Supported by this instruction in black and white, the duty sentry and his colleague fired a volley of shots over the bedraggled bunch picked out in the spotlight.

Moving as one, the by now dishevelled, dirty dozen hurled themselves flat to the floor into ankle deep puddles as bullets whizzed above their heads. They were further welcomed to Winston Churchill's South Coast headquarters by the release of three Alsatian dogs that had a great tail-wagging, jaw-snapping, barking-mad time tearing their uniforms to shreds before they were finally pulled off by a surge of sentries armed to the teeth and in no mood to take prisoners.

'Move an inch and you're dead,' snarled a sergeant as he pointed his rifle in the direction of Melly's temple.

'Why didn't I stick to the beef, bees and beer,' was the thought – possibly his last – that flashed through the Captain's mind.

30

'That will be a puddle of blood you're lying in rather than a puddle of water if you don't give the codeword NOW,' yelled the sergeant.

'Whale station,' Melly shouted back, forcing the words through a throat seriously constricted by a lump formed by fear.

The sergeant lowered his rifle, 'You must be related to the PM's adjutant,' he said, walking forward and offering a strong, friendly hand as he helped pull Melly up out of the mud.

'Safety catches back on,' he ordered the rest of the sentries. 'This must be the volunteer unit. Come on in out of the hissing rain, lads.'

The sergeant caught sight of Private Jennifer Ffuchs-Shafte and Nurse Sheila Blige, who was bursting out of her torn khaki blouse and yet, despite the clinging mud and the rain, still managing to look a picture.

'Correction,' he said. 'Lads and ladies. We've got a lovely pair here.'

The volunteers had just finished warming cups of cocoa when the door of the mess swung open and in strolled Churchill's adjutant. He wore a wide, welcoming smile.

'Well,' he said, 'better to awive late than never. I'm Colonel Waymond Wavenscwoft. Welcome to Woddington Hall.'

31

Personal memo
from the Prime Minister

10 Downing Street
To: Field Marshal Montgomery
Tuesday, 11 April 1944

Dear Bernie,

Just received a full report of the goings-on at Woddington and Roddington yesterday. I know I told you the volunteers should be expendable, but I didn't say lunatic.

I hope you realise, Bernie, that they have a very important role to play during the following few days. Let's face it, this just might be life or death for me... and almost certain death for them.

We are no nearer to catching the Rat, but the trap is about to be laid. Keep me posted.

Incidentally, I want a signed declaration from you that you will not try to publish your memoirs before mine are in print.

Chin chin,

Winston S. Churchill

3

COLONEL Ravenscroft literally beamed down at the volunteer brigade facing him in the conference room at Roddington Hall, the light from the French windows reflecting on his monocle and blinding each member of his audience as he looked at them in turn. He barely recognised them from the motley crew who had turned up the night before, sixteen hours late and looking as if they been dragged out of the sewer. They were now resplendently turned out in distinctive, brand new orange uniforms, each bearing the insignia WC on their lapels and sleeves.

'Wight,' the Colonel said, 'as I told you last night, I am Colonel Waymond Wavenscwoft, and I want to welcome you all to the launch of what we have codenamed Opewation Watcatcher.'

Sergeant Roper whispered out of the side of his mouth to Gunner Biddle. 'Operation what?'

'I think he has trouble with his Rs,' whispered back Biddle.

'It's not the way he walks, it's the way he talks that worries me,' said Roper before being silenced by the flashing beam from the monocle.

'Now before I go into detail concerning just what Opewation Watcatcher wequires of each of you,' the Colonel continued, 'I want first of all to stwess that evewything said here in this woom today is of the utmost secwecy. Is that cleawy understood?'

Everybody listening nodded their head, with the exception of an unannounced eavesdropper peering with staring eyes through a portrait on the wall of the first Lord Roddington, who had built this ancestral home with booty collected from the Napoleonic wars.

'Good,' said Ravenscroft, relieved that there were no dissenters. 'Now I can welax knowing I am working with completely twustworthy twoops. Let me first of all explain just what you are all doing here.'

'And about flipping time,' mumbled acting Major Francis Bigger, who was in fact a lance corporal who had promoted himself with the help of a few document forgeries that were his peacetime speciality. 'I feel like a proper pillock sitting here looking like an over-ripe orange.'

'Sheila Blige looks ready for peeling,' whispered James Kilmore, who was interested only in getting back to continuing a medical career that had been interrupted by the war.

'My bones are telling me that we're all d-o-o-m-e-d,' said Kenneth Tinkle in a stage whisper. As a qualified orthopaedist he knew all about bones, and his were never wrong.

'I can do funerals at a very cheap rate,' whispered Bernie Biddle. 'If you sign up for the undertaker I work for I can get you a ten percent discount provided you can guarantee him burying you within the next year and a half.'

The piercing beam of light from the monocle alerted them that the Colonel wanted their full attention.

'No whispewing in the wanks, please,' he said. 'We

are alweady wunning behind schedule and there is not a minute to waste.'

He adjusted the angle of his monocle so that the beam of light was now directed on a blown-up photograph pinned to the wall of a group of black-uniformed German soldiers surrounding Adolf Hitler. 'You will all have heard of Adolf Hitler's *Schutzstaffel*,' he said.

Nurse Blige raised her hand. 'Is that a kind of apple strudel?' she asked.

'I thought you'd be more interested in a pear,' said Corporal Shorthouse, who was so small that the Colonel could not find him to silence him with his beam.

'The *Schutzstaffel*,' he explained, 'is a volunteer guard detachment. Chillingly, they are better known as the SS. They are Hitler's personal bodyguards pledged to pwotect the Führer with their own lives.'

'Need their bloody brains tested,' said Sydney Roper. 'Wouldn't catch me doing anything as stupid as that.'

There were murmurs of ascent around the room, apart from the direction of Sergeant-Major Bloomer. 'Can't stand that 'itler,' he said, 'but I ham lost in hadmiration for the principle of what those SchutzStrudel guards stand for. What 'eroes they will be if they gives up their lives to save 'itler. There's something for them to tell their grandchildren. What more nobler death could a man hask for, I hask you.'

'Wather the same as my sentiments, Sergeant-Major,' said the Colonel, making the beam from his monocle circle around the top of Bloomer's head like a halo. 'We have decided that it is now time to form a similar door-die personal bodyguard unit for our equivalent of Adolf Hitler – the wenowned Winston Churchill. And that, in a nutshell, is what you are here for. You are the new special Wubble-u-C Bodyguard unit, with exclusive wesponsibilities for guarding and pwotecting our Pwime Minister Winston Churchill. Hence the Wubble-u-C initials on your uniform.'

Sergeant Roper raised a hand, 'Permission to speak, Sir,' he said.

'And you are?' asked the Colonel.

'Roper, Sir. Sergeant Roper.'

'Wight, Woper. Feel fwee to ask anything you like.'

'Would you mind being a little more specific about the do-or-die bit,' he said.

'It's simply that you will – if necessawy – natuwally all be prepared to lay down your lives to save that of Wubble-u-C. In doing so you would be saving the lives of the millions of people Wubble-u-C will eventually save with his wemarkable leadership.'

Francis Bigger stood up. 'Where does one report to unvolunteer?' he asked. 'I don't mind a bit of doing, but all that dying stuff is not really my scene, oh no.'

Corporal Jack Ready gave a sudden shrug of the shoulders, tossed his head from side to side and then let out a cry like a dog with its paw caught in a trap. It was the fit he had been working on since day one of the war in a bid for an instant discharge. So far nobody had bought it.

'Y'see,' said Bigger, 'that's the terrible effect it's already had on Corporal Ready. If we had been told there was dying as well as doing, d'you think we would have volunteered? I should cocoa.'

The Colonel looked embarrassed. 'Oh dear,' he said, 'I thought all that would have been explained to you by the Bwigadier-Genewal. By volunteewing to join the Wubble-u-C guard you have automatically sworn undying allegiance to Winston Churchill, and anybody bweaking that code of honour will face instant execution by the firewing squad.'

Bigger sank back down into his seat. 'That's good enough for me,' he said, slipping off into a trance as he tried to work out how to wangle his way out of this one.

Corporal Ready started to shudder and shake again. This time he was not acting.

Captain Melly raised his hand. 'Can you please inform us, Colonel, what exactly is Opewation Watcatcher?'

Ravenscroft, a gentleman publisher when he was not playing the war game, beamed down on Melly as he recognised a fellow 'R's whurrer'.

'And you are?'

'Captain Melly, Sir.'

'Ah, Captain Melly,' said the Colonel in a knowing way, based on his reading of Dr Hammerskill's report that had been hand-delivered to him that morning. 'I should have known. Your fame has preceded you.'

Melly's orange-covered chest swelled. Ravenscroft had been delighted with the report. The Captain was the perfect volunteer. Mad as a hatter and completely expendable.

'I guessed that I would get a perceptive question from

your commanding officer,' said the Colonel, sending the beam of light from his monocle circling around his audience. 'What I am about to divulge here today is stwictly for your ears only.'

The ears behind the portrait strained to catch every word.

'The sad fact of the matter is that there is a wat in the woodwork,' he said. 'A wotten German spy is on the loose and we know from our intelligence sources that he has orders to assassinate our gweat Pwime Minister. We have managed to pin his whereabouts down to here in Dorset, and now the time has come for us to smoke him out. Hence Opewation Watcatcher.'

'And where is the gweat man who we have to pwotect and guard with our lives?' asked Melly, unconsciously slipping into the Colonel's wurring speech.

'He will awive next week for top-secwet talks that will involve other war leaders,' confided the Colonel. 'They will be discussing the invasion of Euwope.'

'So we can put our feet up for a week?' said Roper.

'Far from it I'm afwaid, Woper,' said Ravenscroft. 'The whole point of having you here a week early is to twy to confuse the spy. We will be giving you as high a pwofile as possible to encourage him to come out in the open. It is our intention to convince the assassin that Wubble-u-C is here *this* week.'

'But can I be so bold as to hask how we are going to convince the would-be killer that the PM is here when he quite patiently hain't,' said a perplexed Bloomer.

'I believe the Sergeant-Major means "patently"

rather than patiently, Sir,' said Kenneth Tinkle, which brought him an icy stare from Bloomer to go with the beam of light from the Colonel.

'Do I detect wancour in the wanks?' said the Colonel. 'That would be most distwessing because, as the Bwigadier-Genewal should have made clear, any dissent or wevolutionawy talk among the twoops will be punishable by instant death.'

The Colonel let this little hand grenade explode and then clear before continuing. 'In wesponse to your question, Sergeant-Major,' he said, 'I must ask you to be patient. That's patient, not patent. This afternoon after lunch I will make further disclosures to you that will weveal exactly how we intend to twick the assassin. We will we-assemble in the libwawy acwoss the hall at fifteen hundwed hours.'

Captain Melly stood up. 'As the officer in charge, I would like to thank you for addressing us in such a frank manner,' he said. 'I know I speak for the ranks when I say that we prefer to have all the cards laid on the table as you have done this morning. You can rest assured that you will have our full support and respect.'

Colonel Ravenscroft looked open-mouthed at Melly. 'When we have more time at our disposal, Captain,' he said, 'you must tell me how you have suddenly managed to woll your Rs.'

Melly blushed. 'I think there might be some misunderstanding,' he said. 'I'm not like that.'

'Guessed it,' said Roper out of the side of his mouth. 'A bleedin' shirtlifter.'

'Bum bandits at three o'clock,' said Corporal Ready

before going into one of his body-bending fits.

Now the Colonel was blushing. 'I think the misunderstanding is on your part, Captain,' he said. All I was intwested in knowing was how you managed to say words like addwessing and wanks properly.'

'Ooh, don't he talk dirty?' Nurse Blige said to Private Ffuchs-Shafte.

'Yes,' she replied. 'And don't you just love it? I think he's just about the most gorgeous man I've clapped eyes on this week.'

'Well it is only Tuesday,' said Nurse Blige, knowing the reputation Ffuchs-Shafte had for fancying anything in – or preferably out of – trousers.

'Don't you just love that monocle?' said Ffuchs-Shafte, deliberately loud enough for Ravenscroft to hear. 'He's made me go all glassy-eyed.'

The Colonel decided it was time to retreat before his tongue got him into any more trouble. 'I'll see you all sharp at fifteen hundwed hours,' he said. 'In the libwawy.'

He put a finger to his lips. 'Wemember, walls have ears.'

Behind Lord Roddington's portrait the uninvited guest was making a note of all that he had seen and heard.

'What d'you make of it all, Sergeant-Major?' Corporal Biker asked as they sat in the dining room at a huge polished oak table eating freshly cooked roast chicken and boiled potatoes.

'Well I for one am proud to have this chance to serve

40

my king, my country and my Prime Minister,' he said. 'It's not heverybody who gets the chance to die for a good cause.'

'There's no cause I know of that's worth dying for,' said Sydney Roper. 'I grant you Winnie Churchill has proved himself a good leader. But I'm not grateful enough to try to stop a bullet for him.'

'I wouldn't even stop a bus for him,' said Francis Bigger. 'I can't believe that I've got myself into this mess. Me, the man who has so far managed not to fire a single bullet or take a single order. My one objective in this war has been to let it pass me by. "You go your way, I'll go mine, missus," has been my motto. Now they're expecting me to get in the way of a bullet meant for somebody else. Not on your Nelly!'

'Imagine the money to be made out of a Churchill funeral,' said Bernie Biddle. 'The coffin alone would cost a couple of 'undred quid for a man 'is size, and I bet 'e'd 'ave a load of following cars. It would be the funeral of a lifetime.'

'Steady on, old chap,' said Captain Melly. 'We're here to save Churchill, not to bury him, to paraphrase that other great Englishman.'

'Who's that then?' said Nurse Blige. 'George Formby?'

'No, William Shakespeare, of course,' said Melly, who had once considered becoming a Shakespearian actor, an ambition thwarted by first-night nerves when playing Hamlet in a pre-war village hall production. He managed to start the most famous of all soliloquies, 'Be to, or be to not...' A young theatre critic called Kenneth

41

Tynan was sharpening his pencil on the local paper, and his scathing review was headlined: IT'S JUST NOT TO BE...

'I think he's gorgeous,' said Private Ffuchs-Shafte.

'Who, William Shakespeare?' said Nurse Blige.

'No, silly. George Formby. I love it when he sings about holding his little stick of Blackpool Rock in his hand. That's one of the most erotic song lines ever written.'

'How can you go on rabbiting about such mundane things when our lives are in danger?' whined Gunner Shorthouse, who was so small that he could only just see over the top of the dining room table.

'Well you'll be all right, Shortarse,' said Roper. 'You're too small for any assassin to 'it. Wouldn't fancy being in Bernie's boots, though.'

'They'd be too big for you,' said Bernie Biddle, who thought almost as slowly as he drove. He stood six foot five inches tall in his army boots, and as what Roper had said sunk in, he broke the discipline of years of long-face training and laughed out loud. 'That would be funny, wouldn't it,' he said, 'if I stopped a bullet for Winnie and 'e 'ad to come to my funeral. 'e wouldn't get in the first car because my mum, dad, brothers and sisters would get priority. That's right, even over a Prime Minister. He might even 'ave to give way to my gran and granddad, Uncle Charlie and Aunt Mildred in the second car. That would be sad, wouldn't it?'

Sergeant-Major Bloomer had had enough of this morbid talk. 'Nobody's going to get shot if we does our job properly, my lovely boys... and girls,' he said. 'All we've got to do is keep our wits about us, our heyes wide open and...'

'Make sure we duck,' said James Kilmore.

'That is true,' admitted Bloomer, 'but even more important is that we works as a team. If we watches out for each other there's less chance of this Kraut assassin elaminating Mr Churchill or one of us.'

Kenneth Tinkle thought better of correcting him.

'Very well put, Sergeant-Major,' said Captain Melly. 'We are a team, not twelve individuals. All for one and one for all, as The Three Musketeers always say.'

'I think he's gorgeous,' said Private Ffuchs-Shafte.

'Who?' said Nurse Blige. 'Old Captain Smelly?'

'No, silly. Errol Flynn. Didn't you see him in *The Three Musketeers*? He can swash and buckle me anytime.'

'Errol Flynn wasn't in *The Three Musketeers*,' said film buff Sydney Roper.

'Well with a weapon like he's got, he should have been,' said Nurse Blige.

She released a loud cackling laugh that so startled the eavesdropper watching from behind a portrait of the first Lady Roddington that he almost fell off his chair.

The grandfather clock in the hall chimed three times and the volunteers were in a happy, laughing mood as they crossed from the dining room to the library.

But the smiles quickly disappeared from their faces when Captain Melly pulled open the library door. They found themselves staring at the unmistakeable hunched and huge back of Winston Churchill.

43

TOP SECRET
Read and digest
Personal memo
from the Caravan HQ
of Field Marshal Montgomery
To: The Prime Minister
Wednesday, 12 April 1944

Dear Winnie,

We Opewation Watcatcher

Your personal 'suicide squad' guards are now ensconced in Woddington Hall, and we are just about weady to spwing the Wat twap.

When this Opewation is over I want you to take disciplinawy action against a young upstart Colonel called Waymond Wavenscroft. He keeps taking the mickey out of me, mimicking the way I stwuggle to woll my R's. He must be taught a lesson about showing us old soldiers some wespect. Warmest wegards,

Bernie Montgomerwy

4

THE reluctant volunteers could not believe their eyes when they walked into the library for their meeting at 1500 hours with Colonel Ravenscroft. Waiting for them inside was not one but *six* Winston Churchills. Three were sitting down at an oval-shaped table, two stood leaning against the wall and a sixth was stretched out on a chaise-longue.

'Wemarkable, wouldn't you agwee?' said the Colonel, who was sitting at the table with three of the Churchills.

'Yes, wemarkable,' agreed Captain Melly, who did not realise they were dummies until he had made a bit of a fool of himself by smartly saluting each one in turn.

'We have had these made specially to confuse the assassin,' explained the Colonel. 'It is not until you get weally close up that you wealise that they are dummies and not the weal thing.'

Sergeant-Major Bloomer raised an arm. 'Just one small point, if I may, Sir,' he said.

'Certainly, Sergeant-Major. Make as many points as you wequire.'

'Well I was just wondering, Sir,' he said, 'how does you think the Kraut assassin will fall for it when the dummies don't move. I agree that Mr Churchill is not hexactly an Holympic hathlete, but he does get around a good bit. These dummies, if you don't minds my saying, are lifeless. They is not going anywhere.'

'Ah, good point, Sergeant-Major,' said the Colonel,

45

'and may I congwatulate you on your wazor-sharp observation. Just as one would expect from a wegular army man. Salt of the earth.'

He turned the beam from his monocle on to the Sergeant-Major until his head lit up like a light bulb.

'In answer to your question, it is *you,* Sergeant-Major, and your bwave colleagues who will bwing life and movement to these Winstons, as we have dubbed them.'

'And how are we going to do that?' asked Sydney Roper in a scoffing tone of voice. 'Have 'em mounted on our backs?'

'Good thinking, Sergeant,' said the Colonel. 'You're on the wight twack. Two of you will each be wesponsible for one Winston. You will walk, wun and wide with a Winston between you, and at least one of you is certain to dwaw the assassin's fire.'

'Ooh, yes, aah, what, well,' said a flustered Francis Bigger. 'I'd rather live to draw a pension thanks very much.'

'Stop mucking about,' said Kenneth Tinkle. 'You're having us on. You don't really expect us to be puppet charioteers, do you?'

The Colonel nodded his head.

'I told you I felt it in my bones,' Tinkle cried. 'We're d-o-o-m-e-d, I tell you... d-o-o-m-e-d.'

'It does seem a bit steep, old boy,' said Captain Melly, surprising even himself by his outspokenness. 'I mean, we'll be sitting ducks. It's not even as if these dummies could act as a protection for us. Any bullet would go straight through and into one of my men. Dashed bad show, if you ask me.'

'And what about your women?' said Nurse Blige. 'We bleed 'n' all, yer know. I might 'ave a big pair of bouncers, but they're not bullet-proof.'

The beam from the Colonel's monocle rested briefly on Nurse Blige's leading points, and then – blushing – he changed the angle. Private Ffuchs-Shafte came into his view, and as the light shone on her she pouted her lips and gave come-on signals that the embarrassed Colonel chose to ignore.

''Ere, just suppose this German geezer has got a sub-machine gun?' said Bernie Biddle. 'He could spray all six Winstons with bullets and get the lot of us. Still, at least that would make the local undertaker 'appy.'

The Colonel raised his hands. 'Please westrain your imaginations,' he pleaded. 'We're not so unthinking that we would send you out without adequate pwotection. Each pair of you will be accompanied wherever you go by cwack marksmen who will shoot the assassin dead the minute he twies to pull his twigger.'

'Ain't that the 'orse that cowboy rides?' said Roper, the Colonel's beam showing up mischief in his eyes.

'You mean Woy Wogers and Twigger, Woper,' said Ravenscroft.

'Thanks,' said Sydney. 'I just wanted to hear you say it. You've made my day.'

James Kilmore decided to join in the fun. 'Here, who was the star of that 1941 film *King's Row*?'

'Wonald Weagan,' said the Colonel.

'And who's that great new boxing sensation?' asked Gunner Shorthouse. 'Sugar, um...'

47

'Diabetes,' suggested Roper.

'No, it's Sugar Way Wobinson,' answered the Colonel.

'Who starred in *The Four Feathers*?' asked Corporal Ready, getting in on the act before throwing another fit.

'Walph Wichardson,' said the Colonel.

'And 'ow about Flanagan and Allen's latest hit song,' said Roper. 'What's it called?'

The Colonel prided himself on his wide-ranging knowledge and was glad of this chance to show it off. 'Why, that's easy,' he said, suddenly singing the first line, 'Wun wabbit, wun wabbit, wun, wun, wun...'

'Enough!' shouted Francis Bigger. 'Desist. This is no time for such frivolity. We're talking life and death here. Churchill's life and our death. Just for the record, what happens if we decline to take Winston for his perambulations?'

'Firewing squad, I'm afwaid,' said the Colonel.

'Oh well, I'm glad I asked,' said Bigger, dropping slowly and disconsolately on to the chaise-longue, and resting the lying-down Winston's legs on his lap while he tried to think of an escape plan.

'You are now pwobably able to understand why the Wubble-u-C uniforms have been designed in such a stwiking shade of owange,' said the Colonel to an audience struck as dumb as the Winstons by the thought of the choice between facing a firing squad or an unknown assassin's bullet. 'We need you to be as pwominent as possible to dwaw the assassin's attention.'

'Well I don't like it,' said Nurse Blige. 'Makes me look too big.'

'I think owange tends to become you, if you don't mind my saying,' said the Colonel, beaming down on the nurse. 'Vewy uplifting. I would say you are favouwite to catch the assassin's eye.'

'Oh, really,' said Nurse Blige, preening herself. 'Thank you, darling. I feel very flattered.'

Captain Melly decided it was time to exercise his powers of leadership, even though deep down he would much rather have been exercising with his beef, bees and beer. 'Right men... and women... of the first WC Brigade, we now know exactly what lies ahead of us,' he said in his best Shakespearian tones, imagining 'Land of Hope and Glory' playing in the background. 'Our role in this war has been clearly defined, and I know I speak for us all when I say we will not be deflected from doing our duty to King, Country and Prime Minister. Who else, once this great conflict that has engulfed the world is over, will be able to say that they carried Winston Churchill through the most crucial stage of the war? Our backs are broad, our shoulders strong, and we will not let the great man down. So I say once more unto the breach dear friends, once more, or close up the wall with our English PM. Let us carry all before us.'

'You speak for yourself, mush,' mumbled Francis Bigger as he unconsciously fiddled with the buttons on Winston's boiler suit. Suddenly his face lit up, and it had nothing to do with the beam from the Colonel's monocle nor the stirring speech from Captain Melly. He *knew* he could rely on himself to think of a way out of this mess.

Bigger pulled himself up off the chaise-longue, clutching the lifeless Winston closely to him like a Siamese twin. 'Permission to take Winston for a walk, Sir,' he said. 'Just to gauge his weight and his gait, you understand.'

The Colonel was delighted at this dramatic burst of enthusiasm from the volunteer he had picked out as most likely to have to face the firing squad as an example to the others.

'Permission gwanted,' he said. 'But please don't woam outside the Hall. We have a photogwapher due here any minute for some important publicity photogwaphs.'

As Bigger marched his dummy out of the library, there came a groan of disappointment from Private Ffuchs-Shafte who was inspecting one of the standing-up Winstons. 'His fly doesn't unbutton,' she said.

An hour had gone and there was still no sign of Bigger returning. The Colonel, training the volunteers in how to walk with Winston between them so that he looked life-like, was just about to send out a search party when the library door swung open. Bigger, forcing himself to look distressed, came in holding a shrunken Winston over his shoulder.

'Ooh, what a disaster,' he said.

'My God, what's happened to Winston?' said the Colonel. 'He's become all wotten and winkled.'

'I called into the kitchen for a quick cuppa,' explained Bigger, 'and propped Winnie up against the oven. Then, before my very eyes, he started to melt. Wasn't my fault, it was the chef's baking day. I'm afraid the heat finished poor Winnie off. Of course, it hadn't dawned on me that he was made of wax.'

He poured Winston back on to the chaise-longue. 'Sorry, but that's one Winston less, so you won't be needing me to parade him around now,' Bigger said, all matter-of-fact. 'I'll get myself back to our barracks and make myself useful there. Don't want to get in the way of your little operation.'

The Colonel walked to a large cupboard door in the far corner of the library and pulled it open. Out of the cupboard tumbled half a dozen lifeless Winston Churchills in the altogether.

Private Ffuchs-Shafte let out an audible gasp. 'The PM in the nude,' she said, adding after closer inspection, 'but they've left his bits and pieces off, spoilsports.'

'What I'd like you to do now, Lance-Corpowal Major Bigger,' said the Colonel, deliberately letting on that he knew more about him than he imagined, 'is dwess a new Winnie in the boiler suit that is on the melted model.'

He addressed his next remarks to the entire unit. 'Let this be an elementawy lesson to you all that under no circumstances must you let Winston be exposed to heat,' he said. 'Even a weasonably hot sun could have sewious effects.'

He looked out of the library window and was pleased to see that it was overcast. 'Spwing has spwung,' he said, 'but the temperatures are nothing to worry about.'

Behind the portrait of Lord Roddington the Second,

51

a pair of eyes took in all that was happening in the library.

Nurse Sheila Blige gave a sudden shudder, and clasped her arms around herself as if sheltering from a gust of wind.

'Oooh, I went all funny then,' she said. 'I felt as if a pair of eyes was on me. Look, I've come out in goose bumps.'

'But, my dear,' said the Colonel, 'a beautiful lady like you will always have many pairs of eyes on you.'

His monocle bathed her in a warm glow, and the goose bumps quickly disappeared.

Behind the portrait, one pair of eyes drank in the sight. Never had these eyes observed orange quite so becoming; quite so appealing.

Clarence Golightly, high society photographer and all around fop, stamped his foot in exaggerated frustration. 'Oh dear, oh dear, oh dear,' he snapped, 'How many more times must I tell you to hold Winston's head up? He looks as if he's had a bottle of whisky too many.'

'Wouldn't be for the first time,' said Sydney Roper, as he and Bernie Biddle posed for photographs with their Winston dummy dangling between them.

The Colonel watched with a concerned look on his face. 'Listen evewybody,' he announced. 'If this is going to work we must make these photogwaphs look absolutely authentic. We will be having them published in the papers tomowow along with stowies about how Winston has a new special, highly twained bodyguard unit pwotecting him awound the clock while he is in

Dorset enjoying a bweak at Woddington Hall.'

'Permission to speak, Sir,' said Sergeant-Major Bloomer.

'Permission gwanted, Sergeant-Major.'

'I don't likes to be the one what pours cold water on your hidea, Sir,' he said, with his deep concern knotted into his abnormally thick forehead, 'but I was wondering, like, if all this publicity isn't going to make it a little easier for the Kraut what wants to shoot Winston to take a pot shot at him. After all, you is telling him exhactly where Winston is.'

The Colonel sighed, and adjusted his monocle so that it was now blinding Bloomer. 'You appear to have missed the point, Sergeant-Major,' he explained, 'that Winston Churchill is *not* here at Woddington Hall. Only his dummies. The weal Wubble-u-C will not be here until next week. This is why we want to bwing the wat out of hiding now.'

Bloomer's brow unknotted. 'Oh, I sees now, Sir,' he nodded. 'Brilliant idea. The Kraut will think the Winston what we is holding is the real Winston and shoot him thinking he is shooting the real Winston. And while he is shooting the Winston who is not Winston our lovely boys with their high-powered rifles will be shooting dead the Kraut assassin.'

'Bwavo!' exclaimed the Colonel. 'You have got it exactly. It's absolutely vital that we get the assassin to show his hand before the weal Wubble-u-C arrives for a high-powered confewence next Fwiday.'

'Permission to speak, Sir.' This time it was Captain Melly.

'Permission gwanted.'

'Won't it put the assassin off when he reads in the newspapers that Winston is now surrounded and protected by crack, highly trained bodyguards?' he asked, shaking hands with his Winston dummy for the benefit of the camera of Clarence Golightly.

'In the militawy intelligence unit in which I opewate we are twained to out-think these assassination Johnnies,' said the Colonel. 'He will think that because we have tightened secuwity awound Wubble-u-C we will not be expecting him to strike. But the way he has been twained to think, he will see that as the ideal time to attempt the assassination. He thinks he is out-thinking us, while we are weally out-thinking him. It's like a dangewous game of cat and mouse.'

'Yeah, and we're the bloody cheese in the middle,' said Sergeant Roper, who was posing for a photograph giving the V-sign alongside his Winston. He made sure he had his two fingers in reverse.

'Wight,' the Colonel said at the end of the photographic session, 'tomowow morning I want you all to take your Winstons out and be seen. Walk him down to the village, dwive him into town, take him wound the art gallewies.'

Bernie Biddle put up his hand. 'Can Sergeant Roper and me take our Winnie to the pictures, Sir?' he asked. 'They're showing *Gone with the Wind* at the local Ritz.'

The Colonel shook his head. 'Sowwy,' he said. 'No can do. The PM has alweady seen it.'

The best thing about the assignment for the reluctant

54

volunteers was that they were living like lords and ladies at Roddington Hall, eating farm-fresh food and sleeping in the sort of plush bedrooms that you would not find outside a five-star hotel.

Nurse Sheila Blige and Private Jennifer Ffuchs-Shafte were sharing a bedroom which generations of Lady Roddingtons had used as their personal boudoir.

Nurse Blige was a little bit peeved that Ffuchs-Shafte had turned what was a comfortable double bed into a ridiculously tight squeeze by insisting that their Winston lie between them.

'What are you going to do when this war's over, Jennifer?' Nurse Blige asked as they lay side by side with Winston.

'I'm going to marry that Colonel Ravenscroft,' she replied, 'have his children and live in the mansion that I happen to know he owns in Suffolk. I'll teach him to roll his Rs until there are sparks coming out of his backside. Then I'll take the gamekeeper as a lover, kick the Colonel out of the mansion and live in the lap of luxury for the rest of my life.'

'Blimey, you don't muck about, do yer,' said Sheila Blige. 'I'm going to become a proper nurse in an 'ospital, and see if I can carry on with a doctor or three.'

As they drifted off to sleep, a pair of eyes behind the portrait of Lady Roddington number two noted the *ménage à trois*.

Nurse Blige pulled the blanket tighter. She had goose bumps again.

TOP SECRET
Read and destroy

Personal memo
from the Prime Minister

10 Downing Street
To: Field Marshal Montgomery
Thursday, 13 April 1944

Dear Bernie,

By the time you read this my dummies should have arrived at Roddington. If you could see some of my War Cabinet colleagues in action, you'd be convinced that they have had the waxwork treatment. I've seen more life in an embalmer's workshop.

I take the point you make about Raymond Ravenscroft. He is the son of one of my old school pals to whom I owe a favour. I thought being in charge of six dummies and a dozen expendable bodyguards was just about the right assignment for him. Let's see if he catches the Rat. Then we will decide his fate. Incidentally, I have embargoed this story, so you cannot steal it for your memoirs. Cheers for now,

Winston S. Churchill

5

It was decided that the six Winstons should go out in shifts. 'If he is seen in too many places at once it might awouse suspicions,' explained Colonel Ravenscroft. 'So what I've done is dwaw up a wota. You will take turns every two hours to go out and be seen with Winston, and each pair of you will be accompanied at a disqweet distance by cwack shots from the wifle bwigade.'

'Permission to speak, Sir,' said Sergeant-Major Bloomer.

'Permission gwanted, Sergeant-Major.'

'What happens if we are happroached by members of the public what is drawn to us by the sight of their great 'ero on an incontinent houting?'

'I think you'll find the Sergeant-Major means "incognito",' said Kenneth Tinkle.

Bloomer's eyes fired daggers at Tinkle from ten paces.

'I am counting on you to use your discwetion,' said the Colonel. 'Don't let him sign any autogwaphs or anything of that nature. An occasional shake of the hand perhaps, but if you keep the cigar jammed in his mouth people will not be expecting him to communicate.'

Captain Melly raised a hand. 'Permission to speak, Sir.'

'Permission gwanted, Captain.'

'If the assassin were to strike, and, for argument's sake, were to mortally wound one of my men...'

'Or one of your women,' added Nurse Blige.

'...say, Biddle, for instance...'

'Why me?' said Biddle. 'Just 'cos I can get a cheap funeral don't mean that I should be the one what's sacrificed.'

Melly tutted. 'I'm just using you as an example, Gunner,' he said. 'It's nothing personal. What I am asking, Colonel, is do we return the assassin's fire or does the one who is left standing concentrate on getting Winston safely away from the scene at a fast rate of knots?'

'Each of you has been equipped with a wapid-fire automatic wevolver,' the Colonel said. 'I weccomend you use this only in weal emergency. The wifle bwigade, hidden out of sight, are pwimed to return the assassin's fire. In the unlikely instance of one of you being shot we will have a medical team on stand-by duty here along with a pwiest to give the last wites.'

'Charming,' said Francis Bigger. 'I don't know about rites, but I do know about rights and I'm sure you're breaking the Geneva convention by forcing us to put our lives on the line for a waxwork Winnie.'

'Are you wevolting Lance-Corpowal Major Bigger?' the Colonel asked, making no attempt to disguise the ice in his voice as he shone the light from his monocle directly into his eyes.

Bigger knew that an answer in the affirmative would mean the firing squad. 'No, I'm not revolting,' he said, 'but I do want it made a matter of record that I, Francis Aloysius Bigger, went to my death under the strongest possible protest. I can be so much more useful to Winnie

58

alive and well rather than dead and very unwell.'

'Oh, weally, and pway what could you do for him?' asked the Colonel.

'Well I could forge him some ration books or I can get him dozens of nylons for any lady friends he might have.'

'Bigger!' shouted Captain Melly. 'You are a disgrace to the First WC Brigade. None of us are particularly keen on the duty we are about to perform, but ours is not to reason why, ours is...'

'I know, I know,' said Bigger. 'We're back to the doing and dying bit again. I joined the Army for some flipping peace and quiet, not to hold my head up so that some sauerkraut-stuffing, würst-chewing, beer-swilling, itchy-fingered fart from the Farterland could take a pot shot at me.'

'But he will not be firewing at you,' said the Colonel. 'That's the whole point of you having Winnie with you.'

'Oh yes,' said Bigger, with heavy sarcasm. 'I forgot. Of course, I've got the great Waxman protecting me. This will make a gripping Hollywood film one day. I can just see John Wayne delivering the classic line, "One wrong move, and the dummy gets it".'

'It is your wight to pull out of the assignment if you so wish,' said the Colonel. 'But I have explained the alternative.'

'Some choice,' said Bigger. '"D'you want to be shot full of more holes than a slice of Swiss cheese by six of your countrymen and know exactly where and when the bullets are coming from, or would you rather get it in the head by surprise from an assassin with a high-powered rifle?" You call that a choice?'

'That is it,' said the Colonel. 'Take it or leave it. Just west assured that we cannot have you walking away from here with all the inside information you have on Opewation Watcatcher. Who knows, you could be captured and have the Gestapo knocking it out of you.'

'They wouldn't have to knock very hard, I can tell you,' said Bigger, pursing his lips and pushing back the quiff of his hair.

'The choice is yours,' said the Colonel. 'You can either possibly die as a hewo or definitely die as a coward.'

Bigger picked up the dummy he was sharing with Corporal Biker. 'Come on Winnie,' he said. 'We're going for a walk.'

'Wait your turn,' ordered the Colonel. 'This is the order in which you will go out and about at two hourly intervals: first, Captain Melly and Sergeant-Major Bloomer; second, Medical Orderlies Kilmore and Tinkle; third, Sergeant Woper and Gunner Biddle; fourth, Corpowal Weady with Gunner Shorthouse; fifth, acting Major Bigger and Corpowal Biker, and last but by no means least, Nurse Blige and Pwivate Ffuchs-Shafte.'

The Colonel pinned the list up on a notice board in the library. 'Wight,' he said, 'it only leaves for me to wish you all the best of Bwitish luck. Your countwy will be very pwoud of your efforts when the secwecy embargo is lifted on this operwation in just fifty years time. You will then be able to sell your memoirs and make a packet.'

He warmly shook hands with Captain Melly and Sergeant-Major Bloomer. 'The vewy best of luck men,' he said. 'I will be waiting here, counting you out and then counting you all back in.'

Both Melly and Bloomer were full to the gills with emotion as they marched out into the courtyard, and climbed into the army car specially provided for each of the WC Brigade teams. They proudly saluted and then drove off through the heavily guarded gates, Bloomer at the wheel. The sentries on duty, who had greeted them with bullets on their arrival, smartly sloped arms.

It was ten minutes later when they returned, just a little sheepishly. They had forgotten Winnie.

Melly and Bloomer were walking along the cliff top seafront at Bournemouth with Winnie gliding along between them when they had their first difficult confrontation. A pensioner from Halifax, who was on a convalescence following a nervous breakdown, turned and followed them for a hundred yards after they had passed him as he came out of his rest home. 'Ee bah gum,' he called. 'Just a minute. Ain't that England's Greatest Living Englishman?'

Bloomer looked around to see if he could catch a glimpse of George Formby.

The pensioner quickened his pace and came around in front of them, forcing them to stop. 'It is 'n' all,' he said. 'Well I'll go to t'foot of our stairs. Wait until I tell 'em at 'ome in 'alifax. 'Ow are you Winnie, lad? Getting a whiff of sea air, are you?'

The quick-thinking Bloomer put a hand into Winnie's back just below the shoulder blades and pushed so that it looked as if he was nodding.

'That's greet,' said the man from Halifax. 'It'll do thee t'world of good. There's summat I've been wanting to ask you ever since this business with 'itler started.'

He moved closer and stood directly in front of Winston. 'What I want to know,' he said as casually as if speaking to the PM over the garden wall, 'is why did you call oop our Albert when everybody in 'alifax could have told you he 'ad flat feet...?'

Captain Melly decided that was enough. 'I'm terribly sorry, Sir,' he said, 'but the Prime Minister has had a very demanding meeting at Roddington Hall, and we need to get him back for another session this evening.'

'Oh, pardon me for breathing,' said the pensioner, suddenly into a personality change that everybody in Halifax knew made him a man to avoid. 'Just because he's t'man in number ten makes him think he can walk all over us. Well I fought on t'Somme up to my ankles in mook and bullets, and I'm as good as 'im any day.'

It dawned on Melly that this just might be a clever ruse by the Nazi assassin to catch them with their defences down. They had all been expecting a bullet from long range, but just supposing he elected to strike from close quarters?

He decided to test him. '*Haben Sie einen Cigaretten, mein Freund?*' he asked in faltering *Schuledeutsch* that he had learnt at grammar school in Somerset.

The reaction of the pensioner was dramatic. His eyes bulged, and then he started screaming at the top of his voice. 'The Nazis are trying to kidnap Winston Churchill,' he shouted. 'Help! Help!'

As members of the Rifle Brigade, camouflaged as trees and lampposts, came stumbling on to the scene, slowed down by their disguises, the pensioner, armed with a walking sticking, made a wild lunge at Melly in a bid to free the man that he, quite understandably, thought was the captive Prime Minister. In the ensuing struggle, Winston was pushed backwards over the waist-high cliff top wall, and everybody stopped and looked on open mouthed as the PM bounced and crashed head over heels down the cliff and splintered into a hundred pieces on the rocks below. The pensioner fainted when he saw Winston Churchill's head come away from the rest of his body and roll into the sea.

By the time the pensioner from Halifax had recovered and then passed on the story of his amazing adventure to his fellow residents back at the rest home, rumours were already sweeping through Hampshire and Dorset that Winston Churchill had been killed by enemy agents. Before the day was out, the entire country was buzzing with the unconfirmed news that the Prime Minister had been assassinated. In Berlin, Hitler was reported to be dancing in his bunker.

It got to the point where the real Churchill had to go on the wireless and insist that rumours of his demise were greatly exaggerated. He made the broadcast from Downing Street, but told listeners that he was speaking from Roddington in Dorset so that Operation Ratcatcher was not compromised.

In a rest home in Bournemouth, a pensioner from Halifax was telling his fellow residents that the man speaking to them on the wireless was an imposter. 'I'm

63

telling thee that I saw t'real Winston Churchill lose his head at t'bottom of t'cliff,' he insisted.

Back at Roddington Hall, Melly and Bloomer were explaining away the incident by telling Colonel Ravenscroft that Winnie had been attacked by a crazed Yorkshireman, upset because his Albert had been called up when everybody in Halifax knew he had flat feet.

A fisherman reported seeing a monster fish just off the coast of the Isle of Wight. He told the local newspaper. 'It looked just like Winston Churchill.'

Temporary Gunners Kilmore and Tinkle drove off from Roddington Hall on the second shift with Winston propped up between them. They were under strict orders from Colonel Ravenscroft to stick to the local villages and farms rather than cause another fuss in a town the size of Bournemouth.

'I think it much more likely that the assassin will try to stwike fwom behind a hedge or fwom a wemote vantage point on a hill wather than in a town setting,' he said, managing to make Kilmore and Tinkle as jumpy as kittens as they drove round the twisting country lanes with Tinkle at the wheel.

While driving into Woddington they got held up behind a flock of sheep coming towards them. As the farm hand reached the car he gave a friendly wave. 'Marning, PM,' he said. 'Noice day for a droive.'

Kilmore raised Winston's arm in acknowledgement.

Around the bend leading into the village they came face to face with PC Shufflebottom, who was just about to mount his bicycle ready for his morning tour. 'Not lost again, bee'm you?' he said to Tinkle, who shook his head.

Shufflebottom suddenly recognised Winnie sitting alongside Tinkle. He gave a regulation salute. 'Marning, Prime Minister,' he said. 'Noice day for a droive.'

Kilmore nudged Winston in the back so that he was slightly slumped. He put a finger to his lips. 'Shush,' he said in a loud whisper. 'The PM's asleep.'

'Oh arghh, oi can see that,' said the constable. 'He's normally loike that when he's down here. Switches off, you know. It's the Darset air that does it. And all that brandy and stuff he gets down him. Oi don't know 'ow he drinks like what he'm do. Moi sister Molly whom works up at Roddington 'all says he gets through a bottle a day, no problem.'

He sat himself on his bike. 'Well oi can't stand round 'ere chatting all day,' he said. 'Oi'm off to investigate some strange goings on. Several villagers 'ave reported seeing trees and lampposts moving. They'm do say it's something to do with the ghost what 'aunts Roddington 'all.'

A member of the Rifle Brigade close by, disguised as an ash tree, made sure that he was standing perfectly still and quiet as PC Shufflebottom rode off.

Kilmore and Tinkle and the dozing Winston drove through half a dozen villages, with just an occasional wave to show that the PM had been spotted on what was his usual route when relaxing at his South Coast headquarters.

'Let's have a stroll across a couple of fields,' said Kilmore as they reached the halfway point of their shift.

'It will do us and Winston good to stretch our legs.'

'Ooh, I dunno about that,' said Tinkle. 'Won't it leave us rather exposed to the madman with the rifle?'

Kilmore shrugged. 'If he's around he can pick us off much easier sitting here in the car,' he said. 'At least we'll be moving targets if we are walking. And anyway, the Rifle Brigade are around to protect us. I just saw two bushes going past.'

'How do we know one of them's not the assassin?' said Tinkle. 'There's something horrible about to happen. I can feel it in my bones. That's all I need, to be shot in my prime by a gooseberry bush.'

Tinkle was still moaning and whining as they walked Winston across a recently ploughed field. He was in no mood to help the PM along, and so Kilmore was carrying him on his shoulders, flying angel style.

Suddenly a shot rang out, and Winston's head was blown to smithereens.

Kilmore and Tinkle threw themselves to the ground as half a dozen crack shots in the Rifle Brigade returned the fire. They all missed their target, but they were close enough to frighten the man who had shot Winston into coming out from behind a hedge with his hands held high. He was holding a shotgun.

'Drop the weapon,' shouted a sergeant in the Rifle Brigade. 'You are now a prisoner of war.'

It was all of an hour before the assassin hunters had to reluctantly accept that they had not caught a Nazi spy but Farmer Woodhouse, on whose land they had been shooting.

His hands were still shaking with fright from having

dozens of bullets whistling past his head. 'Oi thought them were stealing moi scarecrow,' he explained. 'We get a lot of that round 'ere, y'know. Oi were only trying to frighten 'em off. Oi didn't means to hit one of 'em.'

Kilmore and Tinkle returned to Roddington Hall, haunted Roddington Hall, with a headless Winston sitting between them.

It took ten minutes for Sergeant Roper and Gunner Biddle to leave the courtyard on the third shift. Each was waiting for the other one to drive off, neither realising that Winston was sat behind the wheel.

Biddle finally drove them off, and was going so slowly that they were continually being overtaken by members of the Rifle Brigade on foot in their tree, bush and post disguises.

They were just coming to the end of their uneventful two hour shift and had travelled a distance of thirty-eight miles when Roper instructed Biddle to pull over by the side of a wood. 'I want to spend a penny,' he said. 'You wait here with Winston.'

'But I want to spend a penny, too,' said Biddle.

'All right then, we'll take Winston with us,' said Roper.

They went a short way into the woods, and spent their pennies against trees. The Rifle Brigade men inside them showed great discipline in not letting on that they were on the receiving end.

Winston had been rested against another tree, and as Biddle turned to collect him he knocked him with his arm. The PM pitched sideways and there was a loud snapping sound as his head landed inside a powerful steel-tooth trap set by poachers.

Roper and Biddle were trying to free the now horribly deformed head of Winston when the local gamekeeper burst out from behind a tree with a double-barrelled shotgun trained on the two orange-clad soldiers, who were so startled that they both jumped high enough to win the Olympics.

'Oi've got you at last,' said the gamekeeper. 'You'm stolen the last animal from this land.'

He moved closer, saw Winston's head caught in the trap and as he fainted in a heap his finger triggered the shotgun and two cartridges blasted into the PM's groin.

Roper and Biddle left it to the Rifle Brigade sergeant to think of a story for the gamekeeper, and they returned to Roddington with Winston's head still attached to the trap. His mutilated legs were left behind, buried in the wood.

Three Winstons down, three to go.

Corporal Ready and Private Shorthouse were next on the road, and were given orders by Colonel Ravenscroft to drive far enough away not to cause any more disturbance to the local farmers.

Their shift lasted just twenty minutes. The Corporal had one of his fits while driving round a bend, and they collided head on with a tractor driven by Farmer Woodhouse.

Winston was thrown head first through the shattered windscreen, and landed on the lap of the farmer who had to be taken to a hospital in Bournemouth suffering from what the doctor described as Prime Ministerial Tension, or PMT for short.

Ready and Shorthouse returned to Woddington Hall in an ambulance. Both were fit enough to walk, and they carried the wrecked Winston in on a stretcher.

Corporal Biker, who had taken a map-reading course while training to become a dispatch rider, got himself and a fuming Francis Bigger lost within five minutes of leaving HQ. Bigger could not believe what he was seeing when Biker pulled up, got out and asked a tree for directions.

Bigger was determined not to be out for longer than was necessary. 'The quicker we're back the less chance we have of being spotted and shot at by the assassin,' he explained. The one word wisest not to be used when Biker was at the wheel was 'quicker'. He put his foot down to the floorboards, and the camouflaged army car went whizzing round the country lanes at such speeds that even Winston got giddy.

'Well at least the assassin won't be able to get a shot in on us at this speed,' said Bigger, comforting himself as he brought up his pork and apple sauce lunch.

They got completely lost somewhere in the depths of Dorset, and three hours later ran out of petrol miles from anywhere. They had also lost their Rifle Brigade escorts, who could not keep up with the speeding Biker.

'There's only one thing for it,' said Bigger. 'We'll have to get a bus back to Roddington. I don't believe this, I really don't.'

With Winston between them, they walked a mile to

the nearest bus stop. It was an hour before a bus chugged into view, and there was a further ten minutes of arguing with the conductor about whether Winston should be classed as baggage or as a passenger. After reaching a compromise and agreeing to pay half price for the PM, they were at last on their way back to Roddington Hall.

Suppertime had been and gone before they approached the Roddington stop. Bigger rang the bell, and he and Biker guided Winston to the platform ready to get off. The bus swerved to avoid a cat, and as they staggered they lost contact with Winston. He fell off the back of the bus right into the path of a following combine harvester.

The front and back wheels of the giant vehicle rolled over the PM, and when Bigger and Biker walked back into Roddington Hall they were carrying a Winston that was flatter than a pancake.

Colonel Ravenscroft, who had been organising a search party, said that he had never felt so deflated.

It was nine o'clock in the evening before Nurse Blige and Private Ffuchs-Shafte left on the final shift. All fifty men in the Rifle Brigade volunteered to follow them.

The Colonel ordered them not to travel any farther than the village of Roddington, and to call in at the village pub for a drink just in case the German agent was taking a break while getting local knowledge.

'I don't think women should be seen going into a pub on their own,' said Nurse Blige as she crashed the gears leaving the courtyard. She had only been taught to drive three weeks earlier by Roper the Groper, who had made her put his gear stick in some very strange positions.

'Why's that?' said Ffuchs-Shafte.

'Only loose women go in a pub on their own,' she said. 'People might get the wrong idea.'

'Well I'm game,' said Ffuchs-Shafte, her eyes alight with excitement. 'And anyway, we won't exactly be unaccompanied. We've got Winston with us.'

'That's true,' said Nurse Blige, shouting above the scream of the engine as she managed to change from first gear to fourth in one movement.

The public bar of the Pig and Whistle was deserted except for the half-drunk, half-asleep landlord and one customer in the far corner who had a pint in front of him and was reading a foreign newspaper.

Ffuchs-Shafte sat Winston down alongside her at a table for four next to a welcoming log fire, while Nurse Blige went to the bar and ordered a half pint of cider for Jennifer, a gin and orange for herself and a brandy and soda for the PM.

They had not been sitting at the table for more than two minutes before Ffuchs-Shafte started making eyes and pouting at the only other customer. He smiled back at her, picked up his drink and walked over to their table. 'Do you tink it vould be all vight for me to join you?' he asked, giving a click of his heels and a bow of his head. 'A foursome is zo much better zan a zreesome, don't you zink?'

'Please do,' said Ffuchs-Shafte, patting the seat next to her and waving a hand at herself and Nurse Blige. 'Jennifer Ffuchs-Shafte and Sheila Blige,' she said.

71

He looked at Nurse Blige with raised eyebrows. 'How very forward you English ladies are at time of var,' he said. 'I am Tomasz Kowalski.'

He turned to Winston. 'And you, zur, if I am not mistaken, are zer Vight Honourable Vinston Churchill, no less.'

Jennifer put a finger to her lips. 'Shush,' she said. 'He is here incognito. He has been suffering from laryngitis and has come down here to Dorset for a short break. We are members of his special guard, but it is all supposed to be hush-hush.'

'I understand, und my tongue ist tied,' said Kowalski. 'He verks much too hard. I vill not disturb him. I vould much rather talk to you two beautiful vimmen.'

'What are you doing over here?' asked Ffuchs-Shafte, fluttering her eyelashes to try to get his attention away from Nurse Blige's leading points.

'I am on a special assignment zat I must not talk about,' he said. 'I vill have it over and done vith soon and zen I can return to the proper var.'

Alarm signals sounded in Nurse Blige's head, but Ffuchs-Shafte was too engrossed in trying to flirt to have any suspicions about the stranger in their midst. She thought she had better ask some pointed questions.

'Do you have a weapon concealed upon your person?' she asked, giggling to make it seem like a joke.

'A very small vun but I can achieve big zinks with it,' Kowalski replied, astonished at how brazen some English women could be.

'Would you take it out and let me look at it?' asked Nurse Blige, planning to snatch the weapon if she got half a chance. 'I have never felt one before.'

'I don't zink zo,' said a suddenly perspiring Kowalski, moving uncomfortably in his seat. 'Not here. It iz not zer time or zer place. I vould only vant to do it behind Vinston's back.'

That clinched it for Nurse Blige. She looked around for a rifleman. Not one was in sight, but she knew they had to be close. She suddenly pulled the revolver she had been supplied with, and gave a piercing scream. Both Kowalski and Ffuchs-Shafte jumped to their feet in shock.

'Vas ist it?' he shouted. 'Vi are you szcreaming? Und vi are you pointing zat pistol at yourzelf?'

He could not believe his eyes as a large potted plant in the corner of the bar started to move towards him, and two bushes and a dustbin came crashing in through the door.

The landlord did not take a blind bit of notice. He was now fully drunk and fully asleep.

It took a full hour of interrogation before Kowalski managed to convince the Rifle Brigade sergeant that he was a member of the Free Polish Army, who was on an egg-buying mission and negotiating special prices with the local farmers.

Meantime, Nurse Blige and a frustrated Private Ffuchs-Shafte were on their way back to Roddington Hall after pouring Winston into the car. He had melted in front of the log fire.

The handsome Rifle Brigade sergeant had told Nurse Blige that he would give her private lessons later in exactly how to hold a loaded pistol. Private Fuchs-Shafte volunteered to join them.

TOP SECRET
Read and digest
Personal memo
from the Caravan HQ
of Field Marshal Montgomery
To: The Prime Minister
Fwiday, 14 April 1944

Dear Winnie,

We Operation Watcatcher

I'm afwaid I must weport a few cock-ups on the Watcatcher fwont. Because of a serwies of unfortunate mishaps and misunderstandings, six Winstons have been lost in action. But not to worry. We've still got plenty in weserve, and we still have five days to smoke out the Wat before you arrive for the conferwence.

On the matter of memoirs, you can wite what you like about this operwation pwovided you leave the Desert War exclusive to me. I have alweady been offered a wather large sum by some chap who claims to publish something called War Crwy. By the way, do you use a ghostwiter? Yours fwaternally,

Bernie Montgomerwy

6

T HE First WC Brigade were gathered in the library
having their late-night cocoa after being debriefed
following the Winston patrols. 'Quite fwankly, it has
been a disastwous day,' reported Colonel Ravenscroft.
'I am having to order a new stock of Winstons, and I
must tell you that they are vewy, vewy expensive. To
lose one is bad luck. To lose two is a gweat shame, but
to lose six in a day is sheer bloody carelessness.'

The Colonel blushed. 'Excuse my wotten language,
ladies,' he said, flashing his monocle at Nurse Blige and
Private Ffuchs-Shafte, who were still recovering from
their ordeal in the Pig and Whistle. 'It is, I know, wong
of me, but I just need to convey how sewious a matter
it is when so many Winstons go missing. Just put
yourselves in my shoes. How would you like to have to
weport to the War Office that you have lost six
Winstons in just one wetched day?'

Lance Corporal Major Francis Bigger raised an arm.
'Permission to speak, Sir.'

'Permission gwanted.'

'Why not simply tell the head banana at the War
Office that the Winston mission is a failure, and let us
all go home?' he said. 'We've done our best. We've been
out there and risked our necks, but for what? I mean to
say, we're being treated like a load of dummies.'

'I've never heard such widiculous defeatist and
twaitewous talk in all my life,' said the Colonel,

stamping his foot. 'We of the First Wubble-u-C Bwigade are dedicated to saving the life of our beloved leader Winston Churchill, and you come out with wubbish like that. I've a good mind to wash your mouth out with soap, or put you in fwont of a firewing squad for tweason.'

'All right, all right, keep your hair on,' said Bigger. 'I just thought I'd test the water.'

'Moody bugger, isn't he,' Bigger whispered out of the side of his mouth to Corporal Jack Ready, who made everybody, including the remaining Winstons, just about jump out of their skins as he threw one of his head-rocking fits which was accompanied as usual by a loud 'wey-hey-hey' wail.

Behind the portrait of Lord Roddington the Second an uninvited guest, standing on tiptoe on a chair, tumbled to the floor in shock. The eyes of everybody in the room looked to the wall.

'What the bleedin' 'ell was that?' said Nurse Blige, the goose bumps making an instant return to her arms.

'Just a mouse I suppose,' said James Kilmore, throwing a side-on glance at Tinkle. They had decided they were best off not mentioning PC Shufflebottom's comment about the Hall being haunted. There was enough for them all to worry about without bringing rumours of spooky spirits into the equation.

'Sounded more like a wuddy gweat wat to me,' said the Colonel, screwing his monocle tighter into his eye socket. 'Anyway, let's get on. We have a lot of decisions to make before we wetire to bed. Following today's events, we need to weconsider our tactics, and I would

76

be pleased to hear any suggestions from the wanks. But please, no more defeatist talk. We're going to see this job thwough.'

Captain Melly stood. 'Your sentiments are shared by us all, Colonel,' he said, then glowering at Bigger, 'with perhaps one notable exception. But even acting Major Bigger knows deep down the importance of a successful conclusion to this mission.'

He looked modestly down at his feet. 'I, um, do have an idea that is quite radical and a little bold. Permission to outline it, Sir?'

'Permission gwanted, Captain.'

Melly went and stood alongside the Colonel. 'The situation is this, men...'

'And women,' said Nurse Blige.

'Of course, that goes without saying.'

'Well we like to hear you saying it,' said Ffuchs-Shafte, who was in a foul mood after failing to get her way with the passionate, pistol-packing Pole in the Pig and Whistle.

'The situation is this,' continued the Captain. 'The Nazi assassin has had six chances to show himself, but he has continued to lie low despite all our best efforts to smoke him out. My plan is that tomorrow we should use just one Winston to bring him out into the open.'

'And just how do you intend to do that?' asked the cynical Francis Bigger. 'Get Winston to shout, "Come and get me, Fritz"?'

'You are not too far off,' said the Captain. 'I will give you a little demonstration, if I may.'

'Please do,' said the Colonel, completely absorbed. 'I

can't wait to see what your idea is. This is weally most exciting. Just like a game of chawades.'

Melly turned to Bloomer. 'Sergeant-Major,' he ordered, 'bring me a Winston.'

The Sergeant-Major went to the cupboard in the corner of the library, and fished out one of the Winstons they had spent the previous hour dressing. He passed it to the Captain, who stood with his arm around Winston's shoulders.

'Now we all accept that this is the dead spitting image of Churchill,' he said, 'and I congratulate the waxworker who made it. But the fact remains it is a dummy.'

'Too right,' said Sergeant Roper. 'My granddad's got more life in him, and he's been dead ten years.'

'Who buried him?' asked Gunner Biddle. 'Was it my firm by any chance?'

'How the ruddy heck would I know?' said Roper. 'It's not exactly the sort of thing that sticks in your mind, is it? I can't even tell you who the geezer was who married me, let alone the feller in charge of any funeral I've been to.'

'Well, I only asked,' said Biddle. 'I could tell you the name of every single funeral director in East London and who 'e's buried that's famous in the last ten years.'

'So blinking what?' said Roper. 'I could tell you every FA Cup Final team since 1923 when Bolton and West Ham played in the first match ever staged at Wembley, but I'm not making a song and dance about it.'

'Gentlemen, gentlemen,' called the Colonel. 'Please listen carefully to what your Commanding Officer is saying. This could mean the end for the wat.'

'Thank you, Colonel,' said Melly.

'Oh, and just for the wecord,' the Colonel added, 'Bolton Wandewers won two-one, and inside-wight David Jack and a woving Scottish centre-forward called John Smith scored the goals.'

Captain Melly gave the Colonel a withering look. 'As I was saying,' he went on, pointing to Winston. 'This is obviously a dummy. But just see the difference when I do this.'

He stood Winston directly in front of him, and then – calling on all his training as an actor – started to impersonate the Prime Minister.

'We shall fight on the beaches,' he boomed, remembering to add just a hint of a lisp. 'We shall fight on the landing grounds, we shall fight in the fields and in the streets, we shall fight in the hills. We shall *never* surrender.'

'Bwavo!' shouted the Colonel, leading the applause of everybody in the First WC Brigade. 'Absolutely first wate. I twuly thought the weal Winston had come into the woom.'

Melly positively glowed with pride.

'Where did y'learn to impersonate like that?' asked Nurse Blige. 'Blimey, it was so good I've got me goose bumps back.'

'I did a little acting before the war,' Melly said, trying hard to hide his blush by ducking back behind the figure of Winston.

'Can you do Errol Flynn?' said Ffuchs-Shafte.

'No,' said the Captain, 'but I can do a passable WC Fields.'

He thrust his face out to make his nose look bigger. 'Never give a sucker an even break, my little chickadee,' he said in a perfect take-off of WC Fields.

'Wemarkable,' said the Colonel, who then chuckled. 'Must wemember not to get the two WCs mixed up, what? How about Fwanklin D Woosevelt. Can you do him?'

Melly sat on a straight-backed chair as if in a wheelchair. 'I pledge you,' he said in his best Harvard accent, 'and I pledge myself to a New Deal for the American people.'

The Colonel applauded. 'Quite terwific' he said. 'That was the Pwesident to a T.'

Gunner Shorthouse raised an arm. 'Permission to speak, Sir.'

'Permission gwanted, whoever and wherever you are,' said the Colonel, unable to see Shorthouse who was sunk into one of the plush armchairs dotted around the library.

Shorthouse stood up. 'I can do Harry Lauder, Sir,' he said, and started to sing in a strong Scottish accent. 'Keep right on to the end of the road, keep right on to the end. If the road be long...'

The entire First WC Brigade joined in with him, until they were silenced by a loud knocking on the ceiling.

Kilmore and Tinkle both turned white as they looked up, and Nurse Blige's goose bumps came back with a vengeance.

'Shut that bloody racket up or it'll be the end of the road for all of you!' came the voice above them of the Rifle Brigade sergeant. 'Some of us are trying to get some sleep up here.'

The Colonel regained control of the meeting. 'The chap's absolutely wight,' he said. 'We got a bit carwied away there. Captain Melly, please continue to tell us about your plan.'

Ffuchs-Shafte had made a careful note of where the voice upstairs had come from. 'Permission to retire please, Sir,' she said, forcing a yawn and stretching.

'Oh all wight, if you must,' said the Colonel. 'Nurse Blige can fill you in on what we decide in the morning. Over to you, Captain.'

As Ffuchs-Shafte, thinking how she could be filled in tonight, almost skipped out of the room, Captain Melly ducked behind Winston and gave another perfect demonstration of the Churchill voice.

'I have nothing to offer,' he quoted, 'but blood, toil, tears and sweat.'

'Yes, quite bwilliant again,' said the Colonel.

Melly now stood alongside Winston. 'You see the difference it makes when Churchill's voice comes from the dummy,' he said. 'It brings him to life and makes him much more believable.'

Sergeant-Major Bloomer was on his feet. 'Permission to speak, Sir.'

'Permission gwanted, Sergeant-Major.'

'I don't wants to be the one what throws cold water on whatever hidea the Captain has in mind,' he said, 'but I feels I 'as to point out that Winston's lips, Sir, they does not move.'

'That's a good point, Sergeant-Major,' said the Colonel. 'Must admit that the thought hadn't cwossed

81

my mind. What do you say, Captain? Does this weck the plan?'

'Well I think it's rather splitting hairs,' said an obviously hurt Melly, throwing a black look in the direction of Bloomer. 'If the Sergeant-Major would just be patient, I will enlarge on my theory so that you get the complete picture before anybody else tries to sabotage what is a perfectly sound idea.'

'Bloomer made a right bloomer there,' said Roper in a whispered aside to Bernie Biddle, who had a hand over his mouth suppressing a giggle.

'Sorry to have hinterrupted,' said an embarrassed Bloomer. 'I was being preserved.'

'I think what the Sergeant-Major actually means, Sir, is presumptuous,' said Tinkle.

Bloomer was too lost in his own embarrassment to even bother with a threatening look at Clever Dick Tinkle. 'I'll get you in my own sweet time, nancy boy,' he vowed silently to himself.

'Please, evewybody,' pleaded the Colonel. 'It's getting widiculously late and I want us to have something settled before we all go up the little wooden hill to dweamland. Captain, please continue.'

'Thank you,' said Melly. 'What I am suggesting is that we take Winston into Bournemouth town centre tomorrow just after midday. Parade him around and make sure everybody knows he is there. Then he can stand on the town hall steps and make a speech, although, of course, it will be me making the speech for him through a megaphone that we can set up behind him.'

'On what theme?' asked the Colonel.

'On what theme what?' said the Captain.

'On what theme will you make the speech, of course? You can't go putting just any old words into the Pwime Minister's mouth. Whatever he says is weported all awound the world. I think I would need to get it cweared by the War Office. Exactly what words will you be weading out?'

'Oh, I don't know,' said the Captain, irritably. 'I'll write a speech over breakfast.'

'Jolly good show,' said the Colonel. 'Carry on, Captain.'

'While Winston is making his speech,' explained Melly, 'he will be a sitting, or rather a standing, target for the Nazi marksman. Our Rifle Brigade boys can scour the skyline and every nook and cranny to see if the assassin shows himself. The very moment he pops up... B-a-n-g! B-a-n-g!'

The Captain's accurate impersonation of the sound of gun fire was so sudden and unexpected that the dozing Francis Bigger fell off his chair. So, too, did the unseen eavesdropper.

The Colonel glared at the wall. 'That wat is weally westless tonight,' he said. 'I think we must be keeping him awake. Let's call it a day now, and be nice and fwesh and weady for action tomowow.'

He shook Captain Melly by the hand. 'It's a jolly good wheeze of yours, Captain. I'll get the wifle bwigade bwiefed first thing in the morning while you're witing Winston's speech. But make sure it's not contwoversial, and then I won't have to get it cweared

83

by the War Office.'

The Colonel was just putting his sheaf of briefing notes into his case when Sergeant Roper approached, a triumphant gleam in his eye.

'Permission to speak, Sir,' he said.

'Permission gwanted, Sergeant,' the Colonel said, stifling a yawn. 'But please make it quick because I am vewy, vewy weawy.'

'Well, Sir,' said Roper. 'It was two-nil, not two-one.'

'What was?'

'The first FA Cup Final at Wembley. Bolton Wanderers two, West Ham United nil.'

'Uh, well done Woper,' the Colonel said. 'Vewy observant of you. I just wanted to see if anybody would spot my delibewate mistake.'

As they filed out of the library to go to their bedrooms, the uninvited guest left by a secret exit and went off to make notes on all that had been discussed. He decided that the discussion about Bolton and West Ham must have been some sort of hidden code.

Kilmore and Tinkle, sharing the Blue bedroom in the west wing, discussed their day as they lay in bed. 'What amazes me,' said Kilmore, 'is the way old Smelly is ready to put his life on the line by standing directly behind Winston reading the speech.'

'The man must be stark raving mad,' said Tinkle. 'If I were him I would want a wall between me and Winston. Come to think of it, I'd be quite speechless.'

'Well Winston's never been that,' said Kilmore. 'He makes so many speeches I'm surprised he's got time to think about the war. I wonder if he employs a ghostwriter?'

'Dunno. But talking of ghosts, there were some funny goings-on in the library tonight. All that scraping and thumping behind the wall. D'you think it was the ghost of Roddington Hall?'

'I'm too frightened to even think about it. Do you believe in ghosts?'

'No, don't be silly. Once somebody's dead and gone that's it. All over. Finished. End of the line. Nobody can convince me that people come back from the dead to haunt you.'

They were suddenly interrupted by a thumping sound behind the bedroom wall, followed by a quiet, low moaning.

'What was that?' said Kilmore, sitting up and looking wide eyed around the darkened room.

'It's just the wind, probably,' said Tinkle, sounding more reassuring than he felt.

The groan had now grown into a wail and Kilmore and Tinkle threw their arms around each other in the double bed that they were sharing.

'Now do you believe in ghosts?' said Kilmore.

'Well,' said Tinkle, his teeth chattering, 'I've never heard a wailing sound like that before. It can only be coming from the other side.'

In the adjoining Red bedroom, Ffuchs-Shafte and the Rifle Brigade sergeant were having a whale of a time.

Personal memo
from the Prime Minister

10 Downing Street
To: Field Marshal Montgomery
Sunday, 16 April 1944

Dear Bernie,

What are they playing at down at Roddington? Every hour on the hour rumours reach me of my demise. They are supposed to be saving my life, not sacrificing it. And while all this goes on the Rat is still at large, and no doubt lying in wait behind some Dorset hedgerow ready to blow my brains out. Shake them up, Bernie, or I will have your balls for garters.

As for the memoirs, let me assure you that I do not need a ghostwriter. I am prepared to help you write yours at a shilling a word. I suppose you will call your book The Desert Rat. But at this moment in time I am more concerned about the Roddington Rat. Pull your finger out. Best wishes,

Winston S. Churchill

E VEN in her white mobcap and ill-fitting maid's uniform, Molly Shufflebottom was the image of her village bobby brother. She was nearly as tall at six foot three, and her feet, cushioned in size twelve black plimsolls, were as big as his. A major difference was that she had more of a moustache.

She was on breakfast duty, and was not having a very good morning. Colonel Ravenscroft had complained just because she dropped his kipper and didn't brush it before putting it back on his plate. She thought he was most unreasonable not to accept that the flagstone floor had been mopped only the previous evening. Captain Melly had moaned when she spilled a pitcher of milk on to some silly notes that he was making, and he mumbled something about, 'Winston will not be able to read it.' Then the wretched Corporal Jack Ready had thrown a fit just as she was passing with a pot of hot coffee. It startled her so much that she poured it into Francis Bigger's lap.

'Never mind, Molly,' said the nice Gunner Kilmore. 'Things can only get better. We met your brother in the village yesterday.'

'Which one were that, zur? Oi've got noine of 'em.'

'The village policeman.'

'Oh, 'im. The black sheep.'

'He was telling us that this Hall is supposed to be haunted.'

The sudden silence in the breakfast room could have been measured in fathoms. Even the eyes looking on from behind the portrait of Lady Roddington the Third were stilled.

'It 'as been for more than a century, zur,' said Molly. 'Oi've seen the ghost of Roddington 'all many toimes. He drifts in and out as though he owns the place, which he used to, you know.'

'Oh really?' said Kilmore.

'No, O'Riley,' said Molly. 'He were an Irish farmer, who won this place in a game of cards with the second Lord Roddington. It's said that his Lordship had him brutally murdered in the west wing and claimed the 'all back.'

Kilmore gulped. 'Where and how was he murdered?' he asked, not really sure that he wanted to know the answer.

'He were found 'anging in the Blue bedroom. Suicide were the verdict of the coroner, but as the coroner were the uncle of Lord Roddington the verdict were not believed by the local village folk, particularly as he were found 'anging by his feet.'

'But how could he have died hanging by his feet?' said a sceptical Kenneth Tinkle.

'Oh, didn't I tell 'ee,' said Molly, 'that his throat 'ad been cut from ear to ear?'

'From ear to ear?' said Gunner Shorthouse, missing his mouth with a spoonful of porridge.

'That's roight, from 'ere to 'ere,' said Molly, dramatically miming a cutting stroke from left ear to right ear.

Tinkle pushed his plate of kidneys and mushrooms away from him.

'How do you know that the ghost is O'Riley?' asked Nurse Blige. 'Could be anybody's ghost.'

'Well when oi first see 'im,' said Molly, 'I thought he were a noice friendly ghost 'cos he had a big smoile on his face. Then I realised it were not a smoile but his scar that I were looking at.'

'Cancel my fwied tomatoes, Molly,' said Colonel Ravenscroft. 'I'll make do with ceweal.'

'Why is he 'aunting the 'all?' asked Bernie Biddle. 'I could 'ave arranged a nice funeral for him that would 'ave laid him to a peaceful rest. When we give somebody a funeral we always go out of our way to make it the best day of their life.'

'It's said that the ghost of O'Riley has vowed revenge on Lord Roddington and all his descendants,' said Molly. 'Every Lord Roddington since has been driven as mad as a tom cat with his testicles on foire.'

The eyes of the men in the room watered over their breakfast.

'Tell me,' said Tinkle, 'does this ghost of O'Riley make a noise like this?'

He let out a wailing sound like he and Kilmore had heard in their bedroom.

'Oooh, that's made my goose bumps come back,' said Nurse Blige.

Ffuchs-Shafte looked across the breakfast room at the Rifle Brigade sergeant and pouted her lips.

'That sounds more loike our cow when it's in labour,' said Molly. 'Didn't I tell 'ee that O'Riley were a deaf mute? Never uttered a sound in his life, nor 'as he since to the best of my knowledge.'

'So what card game were they playing when he won the Hall?' asked Roper.

'I think it were snap,' said Molly.

'But he would need to have shouted "snap" to win,' snapped Roper. 'But you've told us the geezer was speechless.'

'Oh arrgh,' Molly said. 'but in this particular game he 'ad 'is sheep dog sitting alongside him, and he snapped every time O'Riley kicked his behoind.'

'That his a shaggy dog story if hever I've 'eard one,' said Sergeant-Major Bloomer. 'You'll be telling us next that the sheep dog what helped win the game of cards haunts the hall along with Mr O'Riley.'

'Oh, didn't I tell 'ee?' said Molly, pausing on her way back to the kitchen, 'The sheep dog is always at his soide. He's the one that makes that terrible sort of wailing sound.'

Kilmore and Tinkle looked at each other, and both silently made up their minds to request a change of bedroom.

'That's enough about ghosts,' said Captain Melly. 'Let's get back to reality. I've written a script for Winston, and I want you all to hear it so that you know exactly what is happening at Bournemouth town hall this afternoon. There are some coded words you must listen out for that will require you to take specific action that just might be life-saving.'

'Like diving for cover,' Francis Bigger said quietly to himself.

90

'How wiveting,' said the Colonel. 'I hope you've followed my orders and managed to come up with something non-contwoversial.

'I've concentrated on making it very patriotic, and as Churchillian as possible,' said the Captain. 'I suggest we all go into the library and I'll read it out from behind Winston just as I'll be doing when I'm on the town hall steps this afternoon.'

'Capital idea, Captain,' said the Colonel. 'Sergeant-Major, tell everybody in First Wubble-u-C Bwigade they must weport to the libwawy immediately.'

Bloomer was missing bellowing and bullying on the barracks square, and he welcomed this chance to exercise his vocal chords.

'First WC Brigade, attention!' he roared, causing Molly to drop a trayful of cups and the unseen eavesdropper to fall off his chair.

'Wuddy wats,' said the Colonel, as he covered his ears and escaped to the library away from Bloomer's booming voice.

'Right, you 'orrible shower,' he yelled out of habit, 'Get fell in. By the left, q-u-i-c-k march. Left, right, left right, left, right...'

Molly, picking up the broken pieces of crockery from the flagstone floor, watched the Sergeant-Major march on his own to the library, with the rest of the volunteers sauntering casually after him. 'Oi don't know,' she said with a shake of her head, 'and they says us country folk are the idiots.'

After Molly had ruined his first draft with the spilt milk,

Captain Melly had written his speech on the back of a piece of paper borrowed from Bernie Biddle. On the other side was a funeral oratory Bernie had prepared for his Uncle Roger, who he had buried when last on leave. Melly glanced at it hoping that it might give him inspiration, but he gave up after reading just the opening sentences: 'Our widely respected Uncle Roger, God rest his soul, was caring and friendly but a bit of a rascal. Regrettably he died on Friday in Wormwood Scrubs where he was serving three months for ripping the lead off the church roof, which explains why we are getting rather wet here this morning.'

Melly crouched behind Winston, with a megaphone in his hand so that it would add to the authenticity of his performance. All the members of the Brigade were seated, patiently waiting for him to start a speech that he had carefully edited and re-edited to take out any hints of controversy. Melly coughed to clear his throat and then, in his now well rehearsed Churchillian tones, started to speak, his words crashing around the library walls and resounding throughout the hall and courtyard where servants, soldiers, gardeners and the village postman listened open-mouthed to what they were convinced was the voice of their noble leader.

'This, my fellow countrymen,' read Melly, 'is not the end. It is not even the beginning of the end of the Bournemouth symphony concerts. But it is perhaps the end of the beginning. I feel as if I have been walking with destiny, and that all my past life has been but a preparation for this hour and this trial of visiting you here today at Bournemouth Town Hall.'

Colonel Ravenscroft was nodding his approval. 'Vewy impwessive,' he said quietly, giving Melly the encouragement of a thumbs up signal. The Captain took it to mean that he should speak up, and he started shouting into the megaphone.

'I have not become the King's First Minister,' he boomed, 'to preside over the liquidation of the Bournemouth symphony orchestra. Never in the field of human concerts was so much owed by so many to so few violinists and cellists who have defied everything that Hitler and his cohorts have thrown at them.'

The Colonel made a mental note to delete the reference to Hitler. 'Too contwoversial,' he said to himself. 'Don't want to fall out with the man unnecessawily.'

'I hear that the French generals,' yelled Melly, 'have inferred to their Prime Minister and his divided cabinet that in three weeks the leading players of the Bournemouth symphony orchestra will have their neck wrung like a chicken. Some chicken! Some neck. It will not be the chicken's neck that is wrung, but the bells of the Bournemouth churches ringing out the message that all is well in this green and pleasant land of ours.'

Captain Melly was concentrating so hard on reading his scribbled notes, that he forgot that the megaphone was pointing directly into Winston's back. He leant forward to peer at the next paragraph, and Winston toppled forward on to his face.

'Oh, dammit!' cursed Melly. 'I've hit Winston in the back.'

As these words echoed around the courtyard, there

93

was the sound of shattered glass and splintering wood as crackshots from the Rifle Brigade swung through the library windows on mountaineering ropes.

'Nobody move,' shouted the Rifle Brigade's sergeant. 'We're here to rescue the Prime Minister.'

It took an hour to convince the riflemen that Winston Churchill was not in any danger, and indeed was not within sight or sound of Roddington Hall. 'Well it certainly sounded as if he was here,' said the miffed sergeant, which gave Melly quiet cause for satisfaction over his impersonation.

The Colonel let Melly quietly read him the rest of the speech, and he censored only the reference to Hitler and the very last sentence in which the Captain said, 'If any Nazi assassin is listening to this, we've got your number, mate.'

Melly waited for the riflemen to depart, and then addressed the First WC Brigade. 'Right men...'

'...and women,' said Nurse Blige.

'...the code word in this speech is "Bournemouth". Each time you hear me say that word, I want you to move the mobile platform on which Winston and I will be standing a distance of about six feet. There will be ropes attached either side of the platform and you will take turns to pull at the mention of "Bournemouth". '

He looked gravely around at his men (and women). 'Let's face it chaps... and, uh, chappesses... I don't want to make it easy for the Nazi marksman to get a bead on Winston, mainly because I will be positioned directly behind him. Any bullet with his name on it could have mine in brackets. Is the Bournemouth code plan clearly understood by you all?'

'Understood, Sir!' barked the Sergeant-Major. 'But just one small thing, if I may be so bold, Sir. Would it not be hadvisable, Sir, for you to wear some sort of protection incase the Kraut killer fires a bullet what goes through Winston and hits you?'

'What d'you have in mind, Sergeant-Major?'

Bloomer's eyes lit up with sudden inspiration. 'A suit of harmour, Sir, like what the knights of old wore,' he said.

'But where do we get such a thing at this short notice?' said the Captain, trying to picture himself as King Arthur.

'They has them in the museum at Bournemouth,' said Bloomer. 'I knows because I was there looking at them on my weekend off only last month.'

'What a weally spiffingly good idea, Sergeant-Major,' said the Colonel. 'Twust a wegular to come up with such a wizard wheeze. I will telephone the museum wight now and get them to deliver a suit of armour to the town hall. What size are you, Captain?'

'Forty inch chest, Sir.'

'Inside leg?'

'Uh, thirty-one inches I believe, Sir.'

'Hat size?'

'Six and five eights, Sir.'

'Wight.'

'Ten stone eight pounds, Sir.'

'No, I said wight not weight. I shall go and telephone stwaight away.'

The Captain put a hand on Bloomer's shoulder. 'It's

95

dashed kind of you to be concerned for me, Sergeant-Major,' he said. 'That business about me saying you were trying to sabotage my plan. That's forgiven and forgotten.'

'Thank you, Sir,' said the Sergeant-Major, filling with emotion. 'Hit's an honour to serve someone as venereal as what you is.'

'I think what the Sergeant-Major means is venerable,' said Tinkle.

Captain Melly was quicker to react than the choked-up Bloomer. 'Why don't you stop being such a know-all, Temporary Gunner Tinkle,' he said. 'If the Sergeant-Major wants to call me venereal that's all right with me.'

'Who's going to tell the Captain,' said Roper as a whispered aside, 'that there's spotted dick on the menu tonight?'

Kilmore and Tinkle plucked up the courage to spend the three hours they had before leaving for Bournemouth on a ghost hunt. They went round the oak-panelled rooms knocking on the walls in the search for hidden passages and secret rooms.

After hunting for an hour without any success, Tinkle suddenly found that he was talking to himself in the library. Kilmore, who had been at his side a minute earlier, had disappeared.

'Come on, stop mucking about,' said Tinkle. 'I know you're here somewhere.'

Silence. Nothing. Tinkle started crouching down looking between the bookshelves to see if there was any sign of his pal. Still no sign of him.

96

1. The 'His 'n' Hers' battalion whose aim is to have Hitler's 'herrs' shaking in their jackboots. *BFI Stills*

2. Bombardier Ready (Jack Douglas, right) is under suspicion of having made Captain S. Melly (Kenneth Connor) very smelly.

3. Private Jennifer Ffuchs-Shafte (Joan Sims) enjoys the challenge of joining a man's army. *BFI Stills*

Sergeants Willing (Judy Geeson) and Able (Patrick Mower), always willing and able to shoulder arms. *BFI Stills*

Private Ffuchs-Shafte (Joan Sims) and Sergeant Willing (Judy Geeson) play the pyjama game on the barracks room floor.

6. Sergeant Major Bloomer (Windsor Davies) has something to shout about as Captain S. Melly (Kenneth Connor) skirts with danger. *BFI Stills*

7. Things are looking up for Captain S. Melly (Kenneth Connor) as he reports to take over the revolutionary his 'n' hers battalion. *BFI Stills*

8. (From left), Private Jennifer Ffuchs-Shafte (Joan Sims), and Sergeants Willing (Judy Geeson) and Able (Patrick Mower) are prepared to grin and bare it. *BFI Stills*

9. Captain S. Melly (Kenneth Connor) keeps abreast of things, with Sergeant Major Bloomer (Windsor Davies) not seeing the point at all.

10. Sergeants Willing (Judy Geeson) and Able (Patrick Mower) lure the enemy into thinking they are barking mad.

11. Private Alice Easy (Diane Langton, left) makes eyes front while on parade.

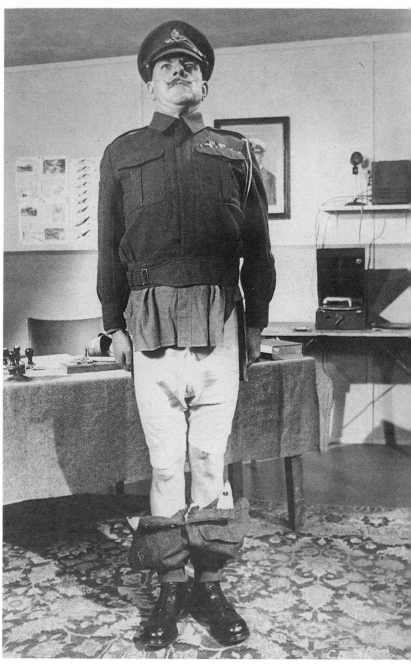

12. It's privates on parade as Sergeant Major Bloomer (Windsor Davies) shows that he is ready to have the drop on the enemy. *BFI Stills*

He felt the hairs stand up on the back of his neck, and he was aware that somebody somewhere was watching him.

'James, I'm going to count to ten,' Tinkle said. 'If you haven't shown your ugly face by the time I've reached ten I'm going to call in the Rifle Brigade.'

He took one last long look around the room, and as he stared at the portrait of Lord Roddington the Second he could have sworn he saw the eyes move. 'Pull yourself together, Kenneth,' he told himself. 'You're letting your imagination run away with you.'

Steeling himself, he looked again at the portrait and this time he was convinced that one of the eyes winked at him.

'Kilmore, you swine,' he shouted. 'I'll kick you right in the privates for this.'

'What's up?' a voice alongside him asked. It belonged to James Kilmore.

Tinkle fell back against one of the bookcases in shock. 'Where the hell have you been, you rotter?' he asked. 'How on earth did you do that?'

'Do what?'

'Just disappear like that, and then be in two places at one and the same time,' said a seriously shaken Tinkle.

'I don't know what you're chuntering on about,' said a genuinely mystified Kilmore.

'But where did you go to?'

'I went to have a leak, if you must know.'

'But... but... what were you doing behind the portrait, winking at me?'

'Steady on, Kenneth. I'm not into winking at fellers.'

97

'Are you honestly telling me that you've not been staring at me through that painting there?' said Tinkle, indicating the mournful-looking Lord Roddington.

'Cross my heart, hope to die,' said Kilmore. 'I think it must have been a trick of the light mixed, stirred and shaken with your very active imagination.'

Tinkle looked hard into the eyes of Lord Roddington. There was not a flicker.

'Suppose you're right,' he admitted. 'It had me going there for a minute. What with that wailing noise last night and the chilling story from Molly Shufflebottom, I almost began to believe in ghosts, and...'

He was struck dumb by the sound of knocking coming from the wood panelling right beneath the portrait.

'This isn't down to your imagination,' said Kilmore. 'I heard that. What the hell is going on?'

There was more knocking, and this time Kilmore knocked back. Rat-tat-ta-ta-tat...

Back came the response, rat-tat.

Kilmore and Tinkle looked at each other wild-eyed. Suddenly the wall seemed to be falling towards them and they flinched and braced themselves. But it proved to be not the wall but a door that was being pushed open from the other side.

Stepping through it larger than life came Sydney Roper and Bernie Biddle.

'You frightened the life out of us,' said Kilmore.

'What d'you think your knocking did to us?' said Roper.

'I thought my funeral was going to come early,' said Biddle.

'How did you get in there?' asked Tinkle.

'Bernie and me were on a ghost hunt, just for a giggle,' said Roper. 'We were knocking on all the walls looking for secret entrances when suddenly the wall on the other side in the conference room just slid open. Gawd knows what we touched. 'Ere, come and 'ave a gander.'

Kilmore and Tinkle followed Roper and Biddle into what was a narrow room. It was furnished with just a hard-back chair which was set against the wall where Lord Roddington's portrait hung on the other side.

Under the chair was a half-eaten packet of oatmeal biscuits, and a two-thirds empty bottle of fresh-tasting milk with a straw through the top. Kilmore picked them up. 'Have you ever heard of a ghost that eats and drinks?'

'Maybe they're dog biscuits,' said Roper.

'And the milk?'

'Perhaps there's a ghost cat as well,' said Biddle.

'I thought I was going mad when you winked at me through the portrait,' said Tinkle.

'Do what?' said Roper.

'When you winked at me,' repeated Tinkle.

'When?' said Biddle.

'Five minutes ago,' said Tinkle.

'It wasn't either of us,' said Roper. 'We only came in a couple of minutes ago.'

'Oooh,' said Tinkle. 'I've got a feeling in my bones that we're all d-o-o-m-e-d.'

Kilmore climbed up on the chair and gauged where the portrait would be hanging. He felt against the wall with his hands, and found a six-inch wide piece of raised wood that slid to the right. Shining from the other side through what was obviously his Lordship's eye slots was the light from the library.

'When our date in Bournemouth is over,' Kilmore said, 'I think we had better have a close inspection of all the portraits in the place. Who knows, perhaps the Rat is closer to us than we think.'

'Let's get out of here,' said Tinkle. 'It gives me the creeps.'

Just as they turned to leave, both doors shut solidly either side of them.

'Great,' said Kilmore. 'We're locked in.'

'I told you,' whined Tinkle. 'We're d-o-o-m-e-d.'

'Pull yourself together, Ken,' said Kilmore. 'Sydney, how did you get the door to open to the library?'

Roper shrugged. 'Haven't a clue,' he said. 'I was replying to your knocking when it just slid open.'

'Feel everywhere on the walls,' said Kilmore. 'There's got to be a catch that we can release.'

They spent fifteen minutes going over every inch of the walls, and could not find anything resembling a door release. For the following fifteen minutes they banged at the walls and shouted, but everybody was out making preparations for the trip to Bournemouth.

Kilmore climbed on the chair and peeped through the eyeholes into the library. There was not a soul to be seen.

They took ten minute shifts looking into the library. Finally, during Kilmore's second shift, Molly Shufflebottom came in and started feather dusting the books while listening to Workers' Playtime on the wireless.

Kilmore got close to the eyeslots and shouted Molly's name, but she was too engrossed in the music of Henry Hall and his Orchestra to hear. 'Hand me that straw,' he said to Roper, and give me a biscuit.'

'This is a fine time to have a snack,' said Biddle.

Breaking the biscuit into a dozen fragments, Kilmore put a large crumb into the top of the straw and then placed the other end through the right eye of his Lordship.

Calling on all his skills as a former peashooting champion of the 34th Stepney scout troop, he took careful aim and fired. His shot was perfect and the flying roll of oatmeal struck Molly right between the eyes. She automatically looked up and then screamed when she saw the straw pointing out of Lord Roddington's eye.

Kilmore watched in a mixture of frustration and anxiety as Molly collapsed into a dead faint. Luckily her scream had alerted Sergeant-Major Bloomer, who had come into the Hall to round up his missing Brigade members.

'Psst, Sergeant-Major,' Kilmore shouted as close to the eyeholes as he could get. But the wireless was still blaring, and Bloomer was giving all his attention to reviving Molly Shufflebottom.

Kilmore took another small chunk of biscuit and fitted it into the straw. This time as he fired, he also tipped the remains of the milk bottle through his Lordship's eyeholes.

The piece of oatmeal hit Bloomer in the left ear, and as he turned he saw that the portrait of Lord Roddington was crying.

'It's a bloody miracle,' said the Sergeant-Major. 'I wouldn't have believed it if I hadn't seen it with my own eyes. His Lordship is crying, and over spilt milk by the looks of it.'

Molly had come round, and was sitting up. 'It's the ghost of Roddington 'all,' she exclaimed. 'He's even making the painting of Lord Roddington suffer for what he did to 'im.'

Henry Hall's Orchestra came to the end of their version of 'Here's to the Next Time,' and Kilmore took advantage of the lull to shout through the eyeholes.

'Sergeant-Major,' he shouted.

'Blimey, his Lordship knows me,' said Bloomer. 'What d'you want your Lordship?'

'Get us out of here,' Kilmore shouted, threading his handkerchief through the left eyehole, and doing his best to wave it like a flag of surrender.

'Good God,' said Bloomer. 'Now he's wiping his eyes with an handkerchief. This is the most incredible thing what I have ever seen.'

It was just at that moment that Bernie Biddle leant against the wall, and released the catch that opened the door.

Molly Shufflebottom fainted again as the four members of the First WC Brigade fell into the library. Sergeant-Major Bloomer jumped as if a bayonet had been stuck up his trousers.

'I might 'ave guessed it was you, Tinkle,' he scowled

after scorching the walls with a tirade of barracks room language, carefully covering Molly Shufflebottom's ears as he let rip.

'I'm surprised at you others letting him talk you into playing a juvenile practicable joke like what this is.'

'I think what you mean, Sergeant-Major, is "practical" joke,' said Tinkle.

Bloomer's eyes bulged to such a degree that Kilmore thought he was ready to burst.

'It was not a joke, Sergeant-Major,' he said. 'We got locked in a secret room and we think we have found evidence of either a ghost or a rat.'

The Sergeant-Major reluctantly accepted that it was not a prank. 'When I sees that portrait moving towards me, I thought it must have been some sort of frame-up,' he said. 'Anyways, yous can give me a full hexplanation when we gets back from Bournemouth. But now we've got to hurry. Winston is waiting to start his speech.'

They moved swiftly out of the library, leaving Molly to worry about how she could get milk stains off his Lordship's portrait.

TOP SECRET
Read and digest
Personal memo
from the Caravan HQ
of Field Marshal Montgomery
To: The Prime Minister
Monday, 17 April 1944

Dear Winnie,

We Opewation Watcatcher

The Wat-twap has been set, and we are highly confident of catching the wotter. We have come up with an ingenious plan that wevolves awound the Bournemouth Symphony Orchestwa. We are going to twick the Wat into showing himself, and the cwackshots in the Wifle Bwigade are weady to widdle him with bullets.

I note that you want a shilling a word to ghostwite my memoirs. You've got to be joking. I'll pay a penny a word, take it or leave it. So far I've only got the title of the book: How I Wouted Wommel. I hope to be able to weport the end of the Woddington Wat in my next missive. Bye bye for now.

Bernie Montgomerwy

8

THE Winston speech on the steps of Bournemouth Town Hall was scheduled for one o'clock in the afternoon, but had to be put back three hours because of the time it took to get Captain Melly into his armour that had last been worn by the 3rd Earl of Boscombe during the peasant uprising of 1590.

The earl had been known as the 'Giddy Giant' because he stood six feet six inches tall and used to terrify everybody on the battlefield by spinning round and round waving a huge sword in wide circular motions. He had never actually killed an opponent in battle, but managed to chop off the heads of a dozen of his own soldiers. These heads had been hung at the entrance to his castle near Dorchester as a warning that he was not a man to be messed with. Avoided, yes. Messed with, no. It was noted by historians that he had one of the least used social calendars in aristocratic history.

Captain Melly stood just five feet four inches, and to say he was swamped by the armour would be something of an understatement. Melly's early enthusiasm and his constant references to King Arthur, his knights and Camelot gradually waned as he sweated and strained under the sheer weight of the curtain of mail being placed around him. The breastplate alone felt as if it weighed a ton.

When he was at last lowered into the armour-plated

leggings and had the helmet, with visor raised, fitted on to his head, he found he could not move.

Disbelieving onlookers were treated to the sight of first Winston and then the armour-suited Captain Melly being carried out on to the specially erected platform at the top of the town hall steps. Colonel Ravenscroft accompanied the Captain, carrying the megaphone for him.

Nurse Blige and Private Ffuchs-Shafte had been trusted with the job of dressing Winston for the occasion, and they had taken particular trouble to get the PM looking exactly right. Gone was the boiler suit, and instead he was dressed in smart pinstripe trousers and black, double-breasted jacket. As there was a cold wind blowing off the cliffs, they fitted him with a dark blue overcoat and placed a black homburg hat on his head. As a finishing touch, a white rose was pinned on his lapel.

'He's never looked better,' said Sydney Roper.

'Looks as though he's going to a funeral to me,' said Bernie Biddle.

'It could be his own,' added Francis Bigger.

Unseen except by expert eyes were the heavily armed members of the Rifle Brigade, who were on the town hall roof and scattered around the tops of buildings for a radius of two hundred yards. Down below, a dozen crackshots were camouflaged by various ingenious disguises. Who would have thought, for instance, that the fern tree right opposite the town hall was in fact the Rifle Brigade sergeant? The dog that cocked a leg and piddled all over his army boots was certainly fooled.

Colonel Ravenscroft handed the megaphone and the handwritten script to Melly, who found it difficult to hold on to them in his chain-mail gloves. He was just about to start his speech when the visor on his helmet slammed shut.

'Get this thing open,' Melly said to the Colonel who could not make out a single word.

He tried to prise open the visor, but it was jammed solid.

'It'll need a bloody big tin opener to get that off,' said Roper, watching the pantomime from beside the platform with an end of rope in his hands ready to pull at the mention of the codeword 'Bournemouth'.

Melly, positioned directly behind the unflinching Winston, held the megaphone in front of his helmeted face and tried to make his speech. All the audience could make out was a muffled noise that sounded like a bath being emptied.

'Sounds like Winnie's got a bad throat,' said one onlooker.

'I reckon he's been at the bottle again,' said another.

Three years training in the intelligence corps had prepared Colonel Ravenscroft for an emergency such as this. Thinking and acting quickly, he snatched the megaphone and the handwritten script from Melly, cleared his throat, and did his best to sound like the great man Winston Churchill.

'Our widely wespected Uncle Woger, God west his soul,' he read, the sound booming across Bournemouth, 'was cawing and fwiendly but a bit of a wascal.'

Bernie Biddle was stunned. 'I didn't know Winston

knew Uncle Roger,' he said.

The Colonel did not feel as though he had the timbre of his voice quite right, and he lowered it by a register and added a lisp.

'Wegrettably he died on Fwiday in Wormwood Scwubsh,' he read, 'where he was sherving thwee monthsh for wipping the lead off the church woof, which explainsh why we are getting wather wet here this morning.'

Captain Melly could not be heard, but he could hear. With the sort of enormous effort that would have won him a medal on the battlefield in the Giddy Giant's day, he raised one of his armour-plated legs and kicked the Colonel in the shins.

This was the moment when a dozen fingers tightened on triggers. The Rifle Brigade men knew something was not quite right on the platform, and they were coiled for action.

The Colonel hopped with pain, and he fell forward on to Winston. It was the signal for trigger fingers to be squeezed, and the crowd of onlookers threw themselves to the ground as the calm sea air of Bournemouth was suddenly scorching with whizzing bullets.

Understandably, the riflemen thought the Colonel was attacking Winston and they took this to mean that the Colonel must be the Rat.

It was either a miracle or some pretty poor shooting that spared Colonel Ravenscroft. Not a single bullet as much as scratched him, but poor Winston was shot to pieces.

Winston was the only casualty. All the First WC

108

Brigade team managed to escape unharmed, most of them following the lead of Francis Bigger who hid behind the tree disguising the Rifle Brigade sergeant. He knew they would not shoot their own, although a couple of stray bullets went close enough to give him an involuntary test of his bowels.

An hour later as the museum curator at last managed to prise open the visor on Melly's helmet, the Captain emerged in a foul mood. He was sickened that his perfectly sound idea had been wrecked.

'What a stupid idea it was to put me in armour,' he said, glaring at Bloomer. 'You were looking to sabotage this plan from the first moment I mentioned it, and you've succeeded.'

'Hi'm really, really sorry, Sir,' said the Sergeant-Major, drowning in deep embarrassment. 'It seemed like a good hidea at the time. How was hi to know that the advisor what is on your 'elmet would not vise properly, Sir. It's surely the fault of whoever supplied the harmour. They should have come hup with a suit of harmour that was modern, Sir.'

'I think what the Sergeant-Major means is visor, not advisor,' said Temporary Gunner Tinkle, rather insensitively in the circumstances.

Bloomer scorched him with his eyes. 'Hi'll get you, nancy boy,' he mimed with just lip movements and no sound. And this time he really meant it.

There was one person feeling even more wretched and shamed than Bloomer. Colonel Ravenscroft could not believe that his attempt to make the speech had been such an unmitigated disaster. He was of the opinion, shared by a minority of one, that he had sounded exactly like Winston Churchill, and he had thought that adding the lisp was a master stroke.

'I have to take at least a share of the wesponsibility for it all going wong,' he said. 'I thought I was giving a vewy passable impersonation of Wubble-u-C. But I think the weal culpwit in all this is whoever wote those words. It was not weally Churchillian, was it?'

Captain Melly pointed at the gaping Bernie Biddle. 'That's the man to blame,' he said. 'He is the one who wrote that speech.'

'Is this twue, Gunner Biddle?' asked the Colonel, the light from his monocle burning a hole in the unfortunate Biddle's forehead.

'Yes, it was my speech,' he confessed. 'But it was not meant for Winston. I didn't even know the Prime Minister knew Uncle Roger.'

'So why did you wite it?'

'Because he'd died, Sir'

'So you were weady for Winston to die today?'

'No, Sir.'

'Look at me, Gunner, and give me an honest weply,' said the Colonel, using the interrogation technique he had learned in the intelligence corps and shining the light from his monocle directly in his eyes. 'Are you in cohoots with the wat?'

Biddle wrung his hands in the way he had been taught by the Uriah Heep character of an undertaker to whom he had been apprenticed. 'I don't even know what a wat is,' he cried, well-trained tears springing from his eyes.

'Don't cwy those cwocodile tears,' said the Colonel. 'You know perfectly well what a wat is. It's got four legs, twitches its nose, wesides in the sewer and bwought the Bubonic Plague to Bwitain.'

'Oh,' said Biddle. 'You mean a rat.'

The Colonel stamped a foot. 'That's what I've been saying you wepugnant imbecile,' he shouted. 'A wat, a wat, my kingdom for a wat.'

Captain Melly, still being cut out of the suit of armour by the museum curator, was becoming concerned. 'Steady on, old chap,' he said. 'I think you've made your point.'

But the Colonel was not finished with Biddle, not by a long chalk. 'I'm convinced that I can smell a wat,' he said. 'Can you pwove who you are? How do I know you're not a Nazi disguised as a Gunner? You might even be the wat himself, for all I know. Listen to this, Kwaut, and see if it makes you feel homesick.'

The Colonel started to sing the German national anthem, *Deutschland über alles*, watching carefully to see if there was the slightest twitch of Biddle's right arm.

It was just at this moment that the Rifle Brigade sergeant was passing by the town hall room where the disrobing, or disarmouring, of Captain Melly was taking place. He heard the strains of the German national anthem, and with the speed and athleticism expected of a fitness fanatic sergeant he came bounding through the door and threw himself on to the man he assumed to be a Nazi, landing like a javelin in full flight and busting the Colonel's nose on impact.

Three members of the First WC Brigade had to

wrestle him off before he would accept that the Colonel was as British (and proud of it) as he was. 'This is the twaitor in our midst,' said the Colonel, pointing at the now shaking and quaking Biddle who was on the point of cracking and confessing to whatever the Colonel wanted him to confess to.

''old on, 'old on,' said Sergeant Roper. 'He's as much a Jerry as Vera Lynn is.'

'Vewa Lynn's a Nazi?' said an incredulous Colonel, dabbing at his bleeding nose with a khaki-coloured handkerchief. 'The Force's Sweetheart who we'll meet again over the white cliffs of Dover, tomowow just you wait and see? *That* Vewa Lynn.'

'No, Biddle's not a Kraut,' an exasperated Roper said.

'And pway why are you so sure?' said the Colonel.

''cos I've known him since we went to the same bloody elementary school together.' he explained. 'Bernie's not one of them.'

'Oooh, I should hope not,' said Tinkle, looking away to avoid the Sergeant-Major's glare.

On their way back to Roddington Hall, Biddle sat alongside Roper in the rear of the army truck. ''ere, Sydney, why did it take you so long before you told the Colonel that I was a true Brit?'

'I was enjoying it too much,' said Roper.

In the front passenger seat, Captain Melly tried to relax. He was relieved to be back in uniform, but just hoped that there was somebody back at Roddington Hall who could help remove the damned helmet that was riveted on to his head. There was a consolation. At

112

least the visor was up.

Alongside him, Colonel Ravenscroft had a huge plaster covering his nose that had been stuck on by Nurse Blige. 'Sorry I haven't got a smaller piece,' she said. 'I've used the rest up covering the ladders in my stockings.'

Ffuchs-Shafte, her mind on his mansion, was desperate to get involved in conversation with the Colonel. 'You've got a lovely voice, Colonel,' she said, as Nurse Blige half covered his face with the huge piece of plaster. 'That was the most moving rendering of *Deutschland über alles* I've ever heard.'

As the truck sped through pitch-black, twisting country lanes, the Colonel quietly sat and considered what Ffuchs-Shafte had said to him. Why was she so moved by the German national anthem? 'Could the wat,' he wondered, 'be a woman?'

The forty minute drive from Bournemouth became a marathon, mainly because Corporal Biker managed to take them on a route that included some fleeting glimpses of deepest Somerset. He was flying at such speed that when barely negotiating a humpback bridge just outside Taunton the truck landed with a heavy bounce and the visor on the helmet shut tight again. Melly was unable to communicate just what he thought of Biker's driving.

While motoring through Woddington, the truck was dramatically waved down by the unmistakeable figure of PC Shufflebottom. 'And just what d'you think you'm doing going through our village loike the clappers,' he

113

said, standing on the passenger side.

Captain Melly turned to answer with an unintelligible mumble. Shufflebottom gave a double take, and then looked at the Colonel with his face half covered with a blood-soaked plaster. With a speed of thought and action he had not shown since his dancing-round-the-Maypole days, the constable whipped out his truncheon.

'Roight, you lot, oi'm arresting you in the name of the law,' he said.

'Why, what 'ave we done?' Roper called out from the back.

'Oi don't know yet,' said Shufflebottom. 'But the fact that this one 'ere's got a mask on and the one next to him looks as if he's been in a foight means you'm up to no good.'

The constable took a closer look inside the truck, and visibly paled as he spotted the bullet-riddled body of Winston.

'Roight, don't anybody move,' he said, his mind spinning at the enormity of what he had stumbled upon. 'This is now an official murder enquoiry.'

He stood on the running board of the truck and ordered Biker to drive, pointing with his truncheon in the direction of the village police station. It was no more than a three-roomed cottage which doubled as his home, but now it was to be the scene, he was thinking, of one of the murder arrests of the century.

Once they had parked alongside his bicycle, he ordered them all out and told Roper and Biddle to bring the body with them. He then shepherded them into his cottage which was full if more than four people were in it at the same time.

Shufflebottom made them stand side by side along the kitchen, the living room and bedroom wall.

'If we all held hands now we could communicate with the living dead,' said Francis Bigger.

Roper and Biddle had laid Winston, his black homburg covering his bullet-blasted face, in the middle of the kitchen floor.

PC Shufflebottom tried to control the shaking of his hands as he picked up the telephone receiver and dialled '0' for the operator.

'Mildred,' he said, 'put me...'

He looked in irritation at the earpiece.

'Mildred, will you shut up about last noight...'

He shook a fist at the receiver.

'Now listen, Mildred, oi'm telling you that oi didn't mean to put moi 'and there. It just sort of slipped when oi were reaching for the nuts.'

'That's what they all say,' said Nurse Blige.

Shufflebottom looked up to see thirteen intense faces ranged around his cottage with thirteen pairs of ears tuned into his side of the conversation, although he was not sure what the short chap could hear with that helmet thing stuck on his head.

'Now, Mildred, oi'm going to 'ave to insist that you put me through to Bournemouth HQ immediately. Oi've got a croisis on my 'ands 'ere.'

He looked daggers at the receiver.

'That weren't a croisis last noight,' he said. 'That were just a grope.'

115

'It might not be a crisis to you, mate,' said Nurse Blige, 'but it can be really upsetting to any decent girl what doesn't want a grope.'

'Chance would be a fine thing,' said Private Ffuchs-Shafte.

'You just shut up,' Shufflebottom shouted.

'No not you, sugar lump,' he said into the mouth–piece. "Course oi does. Just wait until tomorrow noight and oi'll show you 'ow much. Yes, all roight. Oi'll put my 'and there again if you really want me to. But for now, Mildred, please, please, please put me through to HQ.'

He looked directly at Roper and shook his head. 'Women,' he said.

'And men,' said Nurse Blige.

'Hello, Sarge?' said Shufflebottom. 'Can you 'ear me, Sarge? Mildred stop listening in, you're making it a bad connection. That's better. Listen, Sarge, oi've just made a mass arrest... yes, that's what oi said, Sarge. A mass arrest. Oi've got thirteen suspects and a body 'ere in the village station. And listen to this, Sarge, the body belongs to our Prime Minister, Winston Churchill.'

He looked at the receiver as if it were mad.

'What do you'm mean, again? Oi don't know nothin' about him being shot at the town hall this a'ternoon. All I know is oi've got 'im lying on my kitchen floor, and under arrest oi've got thirteen suspects who were droiving him away. One of 'em's got a mask on, and looks loike King Arthur, and another is bleedin' after being in a foight. And they've got two gangster's molls with 'em.'

116

'D'you mind!' exclaimed Nurse Blige. 'Bleedin' cheek. The only moles I know anyfink about are on the cheeks of my...'

'Face, I hope you're going to say, Nurse,' said the Colonel. 'Let's not further infuwiate this cwazy policeman by using pwofanities.'

Shufflebottom put down the telephone triumphantly. 'They're sending two police cars,' he said. 'That's 'ow big this case is. Biggest thing Woddington's seen since Farmer Riley were murdered up at the 'all.'

'But I thought it was ruled as a suicide,' said Kilmore.

'Oh arggh,' said Shufflebottom, tapping the side of his noise. 'But we knows things we does. If that were suicide then oi'm a donkey's backsoide.'

Tinkle suppressed the desire to shout, 'Ee-aw.'

Two black Wolsey police cars, their bells ringing, pulled up outside PC Shufflebottom's cottage within thirty minutes of his call.

The constable stepped over Winston's lifeless body, and opened the door with triumph written all over his face. Not one of his prisoners had escaped.

The police superintendent spent just five minutes questioning Colonel Ravenscroft. He then examined the Winston dummy, and immediately signalled for all his officers to get back in their cars.

'You're coming with us,' he snapped, addressing Shufflebottom, who was taken back to Bournemouth police station for further questioning. It was the police psychiatrist who did all the talking.

The weary First WC Brigade returned to Roddington Hall well past suppertime, and it was agreed to postpone the ghost hunt until the next morning.

'But I thought ghosts only came out at night,' said Gunner Shorthouse. 'What's the point of searching for them during the day?'

'Our ghost,' said Kilmore, seems to have a liking for tea-time milk and biscuits.'

While Captain Melly was having the helmet removed by the village blacksmith, the rest of the Brigade tuned into the final news bulletin on the BBC Home service while drinking their cocoa in the kitchen. 'There has been another unconfirmed report of an attempt on the life of Prime Minister Winston Churchill,' the news reader announced. 'Witnesses say that they saw the Prime Minister gunned down on the steps of Bournemouth Town Hall. Police were said to be looking for a man disguised as King Arthur to help them with their inquiries. This is the seventh reported assassination of Winston Churchill in the Dorset area in the last two days. A spokesman for the Prime Minister tonight issued this brief statement: 'News of the death by shooting of the Prime Minister is a load of cobblers.'

The blacksmith, called out to remove Captain Melly's helmet, heard the news bulletin and immediately telephoned PC Shufflebottom, the policeman responsible for patrolling both Roddington and Woddington.

He had just returned to his village station after interrogation by the Bournemouth police psychiatrist, who passed him sane – 'well, certainly sane enough to

118

carry out his duties as a police officer.'

When the blacksmith told him that he knew where King Arthur was hiding, he told him that he had had enough of King Arthur and his knights to last him a lifetime. Then he threw down the telephone, which hurt the ears of the eavesdropping Mildred.

Kilmore and Tinkle were just dropping off to sleep when they were startled awake by a loud wailing coming from the wall right by the side of their beds.

'Don't worry,' said Kilmore, once he had collected his senses. 'That will be Ffuchs-Shafte going at it with the Rifle Brigade sergeant again.'

'Thank goodness for that,' said Tinkle. 'Nearly gave me a heart attack. We'll sort these ghosts out good and proper in the morning.'

On the other side of the wall, Sergeant-Major Bloomer was having a good laugh to himself. 'That'll show you little nancy boy,' he said quietly. 'When he messes with me he's messing with somebody who can be frighteningly resentful.'

'I think, Sergeant-Major, that "revengeful" is what you meant to say,' said a disembodied voice from the other side of the wall.

Sergeant-Major looked up at the portrait of the Lord Roddington the Fourth, and swore that it winked at him. 'I'll get you, Tinkle,' he said before retiring to his bed a beaten man.

Kenneth Tinkle, meantime, was fast asleep.

119

Personal memo
from the Prime Minister

10 Downing Street
To: Field Marshal Montgomery
Tuesday, 18 April 1944

Dear Bernie,

Another almighty cock-up on the Dorset front! What are they doing down there? If Hitler's bodyguards were this incompetent the War would have been over two years ago, and I could have had my memoirs written and published by now.

I am not sure of the title I will use for my first post-war book yet. I'm torn between My Finest Hour, and How George Formby and I Won the War. I love George, don't you, particularly when he's got his little ukulele in his hand and is leaning on the lamp post at the corner of the street waiting for a certain little lady to walk by. Oh, by the way, your offer of a penny a word to write your book: stick it. Yours aye,

9

COLONEL Ravenscroft, his damaged nose now covered by a small bandage, asked Sergeant-Major Bloomer to call the First WC Brigade to order. 'Silence in the ranks,' he yelled, causing the preoccupied Molly Shufflebottom to drop another trayful of cups and saucers as she walked with her giant steps across the courtyard towards the kitchen.

'Gather wound chaps... and ladies,' the Colonel said. 'I don't want to have to waise my voice because what I have to say is extwemely confidential and vewy, vewy secwet.'

He glanced around just to make sure there were no unwanted flapping ears tuned into his words. 'The weason we are having our meeting out here in the courtyard,' he said, 'is because we believe we are being wegularly spied on and overheard wight here inside Woddington Hall.'

There was a quiet murmuring and chattering among the brigade members, who were encircling the Colonel in the far corner of the courtyard. 'S-h-u-t h-u-p when your superior hofficer is talking to yous,' roared the Sergeant-Major, temporarily deafening the Colonel alongside him.

Immediately beneath them in a secret passage, an uninvited guest listened with keen interest and noted down all he heard.

'It just could be,' continued the Colonel, 'that all the

time we have been wunning around twying to get the assassin to show himself he has been here wight under our vewy noses.'

'Permission to speak, Sir,' said Bloomer.

'Permission gwanted, Sergeant-Major.'

'Is Sir trying to tell us,' Bloomer said, his forehead creasing with intense concentration, 'that the hassassin is a ghost? Somebody what we cannot see, Sir, but what we can only smell?'

'Of course not, Sergeant-Major,' said the Colonel. 'At least, I certainly hope not. What we are after is, I believe, a living body of flesh and blood, somebody who has infiltwated our headquarters and has known our evewy move since we awived here. This is a fanatical Nazi who is progwammed to kill Winston Churchill, the gweatest Bwitish Pwime Minister whoever bweathed. Somebody who is so filled with his Führer's evil doctwine that he is pwepared to sacwifice his own life to make sure his mission succeeds.'

'I didn't know that Hitler's doctor had a twin,' said Roper out of the side of his mouth.

'Permission to speak, Sir,' said Captain Melly.

'Permission gwanted, Captain.'

'Is this why the wat, I mean the rat, has never ever shown himself when we have had the Winstons out on patrol? You are seriously telling us that he has been listening in to us and has known our every move before we have even made it?'

'I have never been so sewious,' said the Colonel. 'The wat is, I feel, wight here. Wight now. Wight under our feet. He obviously plans to stay burwowed out of sight

122

until Pwime Minister Churchill awives this Fwiday. It is our duty as pwoud members of the First Wubble-u-C Brigade to come up with an enterprising plan to twap the wat.'

He pointed a finger at the imposing panorama of Roddington Hall looming in the background. 'There are over seventy wooms in Woddington Hall,' he said. 'It is all too easy for the wat to find a hiding place behind any of the walls. We cannot ask the wifle bwigade to help us search for him because the secuwity wisk is too high. The wat just might have an accomplice among them. At least I know that I can weally twust each and everwy one of you.'

The Colonel looked hard at Private Ffuchs-Shafte to see if there was any hint of guilt in her eyes. She responded to his look with a pout of her lips, and a wink that made the Colonel blush.

'Now then,' the Colonel said, 'do any of you have any bwight suggestions or ideas how we go about twapping the wat, and, please, let there be no mention of suits of armour!'

There was a ripple of laughter, but Captain Melly was too busy glaring at the Sergeant-Major to join in the merriment.

'Permission to speak, please, Sir,' said an uncommonly eager Francis Bigger.

'Permission gwanted, Lance Corporal acting Major,' the Colonel said, bracing himself for the usual complaint or cynical remark.

'If we're so sure he's in Roddington Hall,' said Bigger, for once not trying to be sarcastic, 'why don't we simply stand alongside every wall and shout, "Come out with your hands up, Hans? For you the war is now over." Eventually, if we do that in every single room, we must come to the right wall, and out the rat will walk with his hands above his head.'

'Vewy good, Bigger,' the Colonel said. 'Will you be the one to shout it?'

'Uh, I don't mind if I do,' said Bigger, wondering if there was a catch.

'Fine,' said the Colonel. 'So when the Nazi cwackpot, as he is sure to be, replies with a bullet you will be happy to take it in the name of Pwime Minister Winston Churchill?'

'Ooh, ah, well, uh,' said Bigger, now confused and back into his normal cowardly shell. 'I hadn't thought it through to that extent. If the Colonel doesn't mind awfully, on this occasion I would like to officially, so to speak, unvolunteer myself.'

'Yes, I thought you might,' said the Colonel. 'We need something much more cunning than that to catch this wat. He is by all accounts Germany's number one assassin and a dashed clever fellow who manages to melt into the backgwound.'

'Permission to speak, Sir,' said Corporal Ready.

'Permission gwanted, Corporal.'

'Just how do we know so much about him?' asked Ready, controlling one of his fits while waiting for the answer.

'We have a double agent working wight inside the headquarters of the German High Command,' explained the Colonel. 'Our spy told us a month ago that they

124

alweady had the assassin hidden away in the Dorset awea. He has appawently been waiting for more than a year for the opportunity that he expects to come his way on Fwiday. As dedicated members of the First Wubble-u-C Bwigade we must not and we will not allow that to happen.'

The Colonel looked around at the intent faces of the men... and women... and felt confident that he now had their full attention and commitment. 'Any more suggestions?' he asked.

'Permission to speak, Sir,' said Corporal Biker.

'Permission gwanted, pwivate.'

'Why don't we take a souped-up motorbike into the 'all, and let me ram it into each of the walls,' he said, recalling his pre-war days as a wall-of-death rider. 'That will frighten the rat out.'

'True,' said the Colonel. 'But it would also weck Woddington Hall, and I don't think that is within my bwief.'

'Permission to speak, Sir.' It was Private Ffuchs-Shafte with her hand up.

'Permission gwanted, Pwivate.'

'Have you thought of sex, Sir?'

The Colonel's monocle nearly fell out. 'I beg your pardon?'

'Sex, Sir. Have you thought of it?'

'I'm not quite sure I understand what you are saying,' said the Colonel, his face blazing with a blush that was reflected in his monocle and sending a rainbow beam into Private Ffuchs-Shafte's face.

'Sex, Sir,' she repeated. 'What I'm suggesting is that

we use it to try to trap the rat. Let me stand in front of every portrait in the Hall and do some heavy breathing and offer the rat a snog and a grope. As he's been away from home for over a year he must be pretty desperate for it by now.'

Nurse Blige had her hand up. 'Yeah, I'll volunteer to have a go at that 'n' all,' she said, showing real enthusiasm for the mission for the first time since arriving at Roddington Hall. 'Jennifer can take the west wing and I'll take the east, and we'll meet in the middle, so to speak.'

The Colonel's mouth was making goldfish movements, but without any sound coming out.

Captain Melly came to his rescue. 'That's very noble of you, ladies,' he said, 'and exactly the unselfish spirit I have come to expect since taking charge of the First WC Brigade. But on this occasion I don't think the Colonel and I dare allow you to make such a sacrifice. Who knows, the rat may be a raving lunatic who will jump on any woman who comes into his sight.'

'Well I'm ready to take a chance,' said Ffuchs-Shafte, who was quite prepared at any time to lay on her back and think of England.

The Colonel had regained his voice. 'Thank you for that wonderful gesture, ladies,' he said 'but we would wather you saved your favours for the Bwitish soldiers who weally deserve them.'

"ear, 'ear,' said Sydney Roper. 'We don't want you dropping 'em for the enemy. Knickers to 'em, I say. They can get stuffed.'

'Yes, Woper,' said the Colonel. 'Thank you for that

126

typically honest and forthwight contwibution.'

'Permission to speak, Sir,' said a puzzled Gunner Shorthouse.

'Permission gwanted, wherever and whoever you are,' said the Colonel, looking around to see where the voice had come from.

Shorthouse was standing behind the five foot four inch tall Captain Melly. 'It's me, Gunner Shorthouse, Sir,' he said, raising both hands. 'What I was wondering is why can't we just tell Prime Minister Churchill not to come on Friday?'

'A vewy bwight thing to say, Gunner, and you have pwoved that you are at least not short-sighted,' said the Colonel. 'Cancelling the confewence had cwossed our minds, but Fwiday's meeting is too important to call off. Stwictly between us, it is to do with the top-secwet invasion of Euwope that will be made this summer, and all the top militawy bwass are going to be here. As the wat has not yet been unmasked he could easily go to wherever the meeting is held. No, we must smoke him out here.'

'Permission to speak, Sir,' said the Sergeant-Major.

'Permission gwanted, Sergeant-Major.'

'What if we does just that, Sir?'

'Just what?'

'Smokes him out, Sir?'

'But that's what we've been twying to do,' said the Colonel.

'No, Sir,' said Bloomer, ' I mean illiterately.'

'I think what the Sergeant-Major means to say is literally,' said Tinkle.

127

Bloomer was too intent on sharing his plan to take any notice of the interruption. 'What we does, Sir, is gets smoke bombs and pokes them through the hyes of all them portraits of the Lords and Ladies what is hanging in the Hall. The German rat what is 'iding behind one of them is sure to come out coughing with his hands up.'

'What an absolutely spiffing idea,' said the Colonel. 'Just what one has come to expect from a wegular in His Majesty's Army.'

Bloomer's chest was sticking out so far that one of his long service medals popped off.

'Permission to speak, Sir,' said Captain Melly, determined to try to sabotage the Sergeant-Major's plan in revenge for him wrecking his idea with the suit of armour suggestion.

'Permission gwanted, Captain.'

'I don't wish to be the one to pour cold water on the Sergeant-Major's idea, Sir,' he said, deliberately using Bloomer's phraseology, 'but just how do we get a smoke bomb, which is the size of a football, through the eyes on the portrait? I have noticed when looking at the portraits, sir, that the Roddingtons, both the Lords and the Ladies, tend to have very small eyes. Piggy eyes, you might say. A result of all that inter-breeding, I suppose.'

'That's a vewy good point, Captain,' said the Colonel. 'I hadn't thought of that. I suppose this wecks your otherwise excellent plan, Sergeant-Major.'

The lines on Bloomer's forehead had become mountainous as he tried desperately to think of a way round the problem. Alongside him, Captain Melly was trying hard to keep the look of gloating and satisfaction off his face.

'It's simple. We just pump the smoke in through a tube placed in the eye sockets.'

'Brilliant!' roared the Sergeant-Major looking round to see who had rescued his plan. He nearly choked when he realised that it was Tinkle. The Captain was having similar reactions.

'Why Temporary Gunner Tinkle,' said Bloomer, 'I didn't know you had it in you to be so ingenitals.'

'I think what the Sergeant-Major means to say is ingenious,' said Tinkle.

'Quite right, you clever lad,' said Bloomer. 'Ingenious was the word what I was looking for.'

'Wight,' said the Colonel. 'That's it, then. So that we can talk in code once we are back inside Woddington Hall we shall call this top-secwet mission Opewation Cigawette.'

'Cigawette, Colonel?' said Captain Melly.

'No thank you, Captain, I don't smoke.'

As it was his idea, Sergeant-Major Bloomer was put in charge of organising the practical side of Operation Cigarette while Colonel Ravenscroft and Captain Melly concentrated on the logistics. They held a quick inventory and found out that there were a total of one hundred and sixty-eight portraits hanging in the seventy-two rooms of the Hall.

'Goodness me, there seem to have been a weally awful lot of Woddingtons,' said the Colonel.

'Not necessarily, Sir,' said the Captain. 'I noticed that one hundred and eight of the portraits were of the same

129

Lord Roddington the Second. Must have been something of a vain chap.'

'I had an uncle like that once,' said the Colonel. 'Was always having his portwait painted. He died vewy young, and they found out at the autopsy that he was allergic to oil paint.'

'So he was well oiled when he died,' said the Captain, making what was for him a rare funny remark. For some reason, the Colonel did not see the funny side of it and burned Melly's lips with the beam from his monocle.

The Colonel did his arithmetic, and worked it out that they would need four hundred yards of rubber tubing to get the smoke through all the eye sockets at once. 'We have to fill them with smoke all at the same time,' he explained, 'otherwise the wat could simply wun from one secwet hiding place to another. We must smoke him out in one go.'

'Very good,' said the Captain. 'I hadn't thought of that. All that training at the intelligence corps is certainly proving worthwhile.'

'Yes, I wouldn't have missed it for the world,' said the Colonel. 'It was the making of me. You won't believe this, Captain Melly, but when I first joined the Army in 1940 I was something of a disappointment to my pawents. Pater had given me a job in his publishing house, and I'm afwaid I cost him a wather large packet with the first book that I commissioned in the spwing of 1939. We had one hundred thousand copies pwinted, and we sold just two.'

'What was the book called?' asked the Captain.

'*Biking Holidays in Bavawia*, with an intwoduction

by Hermann Goewing.'

The Captain's eyes lit up. 'I bought that!' he exclaimed. 'I had my route all worked out, starting at the Beer Hall in Munich just as the book advised. I had bought my napsack and a spare pair of bicycle clips and then, sadly, came the war.'

'Yes, it was a wather unfortunate bit of timing,' said the Colonel. 'And even worse, I'm afwaid, was a second book that I commissioned that had to be pulped without a single copy going on sale.'

'What was that?' asked the Captain.

'*Italy On One Thousand Lire A Day*. It was a fully illustwated guide to touring Italy, with a pwologue by Benito Mussolini and an epilogue by The Pope. But that's the publishing world for you. Evewy book is a wisk, and I'm afwaid all thwee of mine were a disaster.'

'All three?' said the Captain. 'There was a third book?'

'Well not quite, but we did pay a pwetty huge advance after I had set up the deal.'

'Who with?'

'Josef Goebbels. We paid him fifty thousand pounds on signature of contwact for him to wite about a holiday he once spent in Glasgow. It was going to be called *Goebbels in the Gorbals*. We did not see a single word. There was quite a carwy on, I can tell you. Pater sent him a verwy strong telegwam early in 1940 demanding either the manuscwipt or the money back. All he got back was a postcard from Berlin that wead simply, "The deal is off and the money is spent, you *dumbkopf*".'

'Tough cheese, old man,' said the Captain. 'I had a similar bit of bad luck on my farm in Somerset just before

131

the outbreak of war.'

'What was that?' asked the Colonel.

'Well I had this idea of making my farm fully automated so that I could cut the huge overheads,' he said. 'I was having to pay some of our farm hands as much as fivepence an hour. One day, it was in the early summer of 1939, I read this article about a revolutionary new engine that had been invented in Stuttgart that could help with the harvesting and the milking. I sent off the million marks they asked for in the advertisement, and then in the September I got back a reply that read, "Up yours, Tommy." It was signed Herr Messerschmitt. Didn't get the engine or my money back. I still write to them every month or so demanding a refund.'

The Colonel and the Captain passed a pleasurable hour chatting away in the lounge, with only the eavesdropper for company. They did not realise the time had slipped away, and before they managed to finish working out the logistical side of Operation Cigarette an excited Sergeant-Major Bloomer was wrecking the peace of their quiet conversation.

'Permission to hinterrupt, Sirs,' he bellowed.

'Yes, what is it, Sergeant-Major?' said the Colonel, trying to hide his irritation at the sudden disturbance.

'We has now got hall the smoke bottle happliances in place,' he reported, 'and we is ready to make the rat cough hup, Sirs.'

'But what about the four hundred yards of wubber tubing?' said the Colonel, 'You could not possibly have got that yet.'

'Begging your pardons, Sirs,' said Bloomer, 'but

Temporary Gunner Tinkle, with a lot of hinspiration from me I might hadd, came up with the bright hidea of filling milk bottles with smoke, Sirs, and then releasing the smoke through the heye holes through funnels what we has borrowed from the milking maids.'

'Jolly good show,' said the Colonel.

He nudged the Captain and laughed. 'Better be weally careful with these bwilliant lads... and ladies... of yours, Captain,' he said. 'Before we know it they'll almost make us superfluous.'

As there were only twelve brigade members, with the Colonel as the supervising officer, it was decided that Operation Cigarette had to be carried out a wing and a floor at a time.

They started on the ground floor in the east wing, and each went into one of the twelve main rooms carrying a milk bottle and a funnel. The bottles had been filled with smoke from an old steam engine that was parked in a barn in a nearby field on the four hundred acres of farmland surrounding the Hall.

At a given signal from the Colonel, a loud double blast on a whistle he had borrowed from the police superintendent, each member of the First WC Brigade climbed on to a chair, poked the end of a metal funnel through one of the portrait eyeholes and released the smoke into the narrow rooms behind.

There was a lot of scurrying around behind the walls, but the only things that appeared were coughing mice. No sign of a single rat.

The brigade moved next into the west wing. They went

133

through the same procedure, and with the same result. Watching from his spyhole in the ceiling, the unseen eavesdropper shook his head, and scribbled some more notes.

It just so happened that as the Colonel was giving his double blast on the whistle, PC Shufflebottom was riding by the Hall on his bike, making his daily rounds of the local villages. Hearing the police whistle emergency call, he came flying past the sentries into the courtyard and dashed into the kitchen. His sudden arrival gave his sister, Molly, such a shock that she dropped another trayful of crockery.

'Who blew that whistle?' said PC Shufflebottom.

'What whistle?'

'The whistle that blew just now. A police whistle. You could hear it moiles away.'

Molly, who had had her head in the oven when the Colonel blew his whistle, shrugged her wide shoulders. 'Oi don't knows what you'm talking about,' she said, pulling a face at her brother. 'Dad were roight about you. He said you 'ad summat loose in your 'ead. Oi reckon it must be the pea from your whistle rattling around and damaging your brains.'

'But oi'm telling 'ee that oi heard a double blast just loike this,' he said.

He took out his 1937 Thunderer and blew a loud double blast, police regulation style.

Over in the west wing, the members of the First WC Brigade, who had just collected their refills, reacted to the whistle by releasing the smoke in the middle of the rooms in which they were standing, and within minutes

134

they were all crowding out in the courtyard coughing and spluttering.

The Colonel followed them out with the whistle in his hands, and his handkerchief to his mouth. His monocle was covered with black smoke. 'Weally, this is too much,' he was shouting between fits of coughing. The only one not having a fit was Corporal Ready.

'Why on earth didn't you wait for *my* whistle?' the Captain asked. 'I distinctly said that I should give a double blast before you weleased the smoke. Now everybody's choking and coughing except the wat.'

Shufflebottom caught sight of the Colonel with the whistle in his hand, and he came charging out of the kitchen.

'Caught you whistle-handed,' he said, getting the Colonel in a stranglehold. 'Impersonating a police officer is a very serious offence.'

It took half an hour of argument with Shufflebottom before he finally agreed to release the Colonel, and only then because his attention had been drawn by the arrival of the village fire brigade. They came roaring through the gates in a 1920s red fire engine that was snorting steam after a fifteen mile an hour charge from Woddington.

'Out of the way, Shufflebottom,' shouted fire chief Jack Puddletree, who doubled as the village postman. 'This is a job for we foire brigade boys not the police force.'

'But where's the foire?' said Shufflebottom.

'Are 'ee blind or summat?' said Puddletree, as he raced past him with a fire hose in his hand. He indicated towards the roof of the Hall.

The heads of the Colonel, the Captain, Shufflebottom and the still-coughing members of the First WC Brigade looked up to see smoke billowing from the roof. All the smoke that had been poured through the portrait eyes had immediately been sucked up by a current of air into the roof and was finding a way out through the guttering.

'But that's only smoke fwom milk bottles,' yelled Colonel Ravenscroft as Puddletree and his crew of five firemen started clambering up ladders with hosepipes at the ready.

'Oi think you'm been drinking too much mad cow's milk,' said Shufflebottom.

'But it is only smoke,' shouted Captain Melly, cupping his hands so that the firemen could hear him.

'Don't troi to tell me about foires, sonny,' replied Puddletree, who was on the far side of seventy. 'Oi were putting 'em out when you were still in short pants, and I knows that there's no smoke without foire.'

For the next hour the fire brigade were hosing hundreds of gallons of water down into the upperfloor rooms of the Hall from up on the roof. They then came down to the still smoke-filled west wing and sprayed more water until the floors were as covered as an indoor swimming pool. Then they came outside and doused the walls of the Hall for twenty minutes, until the courtyard was also awash with water.

A perspiring Puddlefoot led his firemen out after their two hour water show. 'Well that's put that out,' he said. 'Oi reckon it were caused by a cigarette. You'm people want to be more careful.'

136

The eavesdropper, nice and dry and snug in his new hiding place over the breakfast room, watched it all and shook his head in wonderment.

'I said we should have tried sex,' said Private Ffuchs-Shafte.

'Nice idea, Sergeant-Major,' said a smug Captain Melly, who had a plan all his own that he would save until all the water had been mopped up.

His love of beef, bees and beer were about to pay rich dividends. If he got his way, the next operation would be called The Sting.

TOP SECRET
Read and digest
Personal memo
from the Caravan HQ
of Field Marshal Montgomery
To: The Prime Minister
Wednesday, 19 April 1944

Dear Winnie,

We Opewation Watcatcher

Yes, they widdled Winston with bullets on the steps of Bournemouth Town Hall but only because of that widiculous Colonel Waymond Wavenscwoft. While he is in charge of this opewation we've got more chance of catching Jack the Wipper than the Wat. Incidentally, do you know who the Wipper was? Was it one of the Woyals?

You may have wead in the newspapers that Woddington Hall was wecently damaged in a fire, but I am assured that it was just a smoke alarm. I note that you are not intewested in ghosting my memoirs, so I will just have to wite them myself. No pwoblem. I can wite better than what you can any day. Warmest wegards.

Bernie Montgomerwy

138

10

CAPTAIN Melly, his face protected behind a veil, stood alongside the beehive on his Somerset farm feeling at peace with the world for the first time since the lousy war had taken him away from what he called 'the greatest lady in my life'. This was Beth, the Queen Bee, who ruled her colony of bees with a discipline and a dignity that he found both fascinating and moving. It was nothing unusual for the Captain to be found weeping alongside his hive, crying with sheer joy and emotional affection at the beautiful sight of the bees paying homage to their Queen and working their little butts off so that she could luxuriate in a bed of honey.

Melly had a theory that if the human race would only act with the same energy, efficiency, loyalty, dedication, sense and sensibility as the bee population there would be no time or appetite for world wars; and a dictator like Hitler would never be allowed to rise to power. He would have his testicles, or rather his testicle, injected with venom the moment he tried to get too big for his jackboots.

The Captain cultivated a new Queen Bee every year or so as the old Queen died, but he never allowed himself to accept that she had passed on. He convinced himself that each new Queen was the previous one reincarnated. Good Queen Beth could count him number one among her courtiers.

The members of the First WC Brigade watched from

a safe distance and from behind trees and bushes as Melly talked to his bees like a doting parent. 'Daddy's back,' he said, 'and I'm here to give you an assignment that can help make you the most famous bees in the whole of Great Britain. You will be the bees' knees.'

He had brought the Colonel and the WC volunteers to his farm ten miles south of Bridgewater to outline his plan for a buzzing attack on the rat of Roddington Hall.

The Captain summoned them forward from their hideaways. 'You're in no danger,' he said. 'My bees wouldn't harm a fly.'

'It's me I'm worried about, not a fly,' said Nurse Blige.

'Ooh, that word fly is so erotic,' said Private Ffuchs-Shafte.

''Ow do we know the bees ain't going to sting us to buggery?' asked Sydney Roper from behind an apple tree fifty yards away.

'You're in more danger over there, I can assure you,' said Melly. 'There are likely to be worthless drones who have been kicked out by Queen Beth hiding in that tree above your head.'

Roper, a true Bow-belled Cockney who felt as out of place on a farm as a cat in a dog pound, instinctively went into a crouch and moved almost on all fours to join Melly by the hive.

'Permission to speak, Sir,' said Sergeant-Major Bloomer, rather weakly by his booming standards. He was nervously considering whether the Captain had some sinister plan in mind to gain revenge for the suit of armour episode.

'Permission granted, Sergeant-Major,' said Melly.

'I was wondering, Sir,' Bloomer said from behind a bush, 'if you can hassure us that those bees of yours are friendly. You see, Sir, I has an allegiance to stings.'

'I think what the Sergeant-Major means to say is that he has an allergy,' corrected Tinkle, from behind a gate post.

'Quite right, clever boy,' said Bloomer, glad to have the proper word conveyed to the Captain. 'It's hallergic what I ham.'

Captain Melly dipped his bare hands and arms into the hive and when he brought them out they were crawling with bees. 'You see,' he said, 'they are harmless provided you don't bother them. Live and let live is their sensible motto.'

'That's weally impwessive,' shouted Colonel Ravenscroft, who was sheltering inside the army truck with six other Brigade members. 'You have convinced me that it is all wight for us to join you. Sergeant-Major, get the Brigade to fall in.'

In what was probably the weakest command of his entire career – even including the time when he was suffering from laryngitis – Bloomer called in little more than a stage whisper: 'First WC Brigade, get fell in.' He did not want to risk waking or disturbing the bees.

Melly had returned the bees to their hive by the time all the members had rather reluctantly gathered round him. They had always considered him something of a buffoon on the barracks square, but here on his own territory the Captain had, with some justification, gained new respect and authority.

'Permission to speak, Sir,' Melly said out of deference

141

to his superior officer, Colonel Ravenscroft.

'But of course,' said the Colonel. 'Permission gwanted, Captain Melly.'

'The reason I've invited you all here to my farm today,' the Captain said, 'is to outline a plan that I am convinced will trap the rat. As the Colonel said so fittingly a few days ago, "Remember walls have ears." I am sure that everything we have said and planned inside Roddington Hall has been intercepted by whoever is lurking behind those walls. But here on my farm there is no uninvited and unseen guest who can listen in. If there were, my bees would sense it within seconds and deliver a sting that would have a lasting effect.'

'But I thought you said they were friendly bleeding bees,' said Roper, voicing the thoughts of the rest of the brigade.

'Yes, but they instinctively know when somebody is not welcome,' said Melly. 'I am relaxed with you my friends and colleagues, and so my bees are relaxed. Queen Beth would quickly pick up any bad vibes, and she would order a mass attack.'

'Well you tell Queen Beth,' said a quivering Francis Bigger, 'that we come in peace.'

'Yeah, and we don't want to leave in pieces thanks very much,' added Gunner Shorthouse, who for once felt pleased that he was such a small target.

'For gawd's sake keep them in their 'ive,' said the giant Bernie Biddle, conscious that he was an unmissable target. 'I don't want to be stung for funeral costs, fanks very much.'

'Why is Queen Beth so special?' asked Private Ffuchs-

Shafte. 'What has she got that the other bees haven't got?'

'I could eulogise about her for an hour and still not cover all her good points,' said the Captain. 'Just on the productivity side, she is capable of laying more than one thousand eggs in a single day and she can mate with more than one drone while in flight.'

Ffuchs-Shafte licked her lips. 'One day somebody might think of saying that good Queen Beth invented the mile-high club,' she said.

'How come that you're not wearing any protection on your hands and arms?' asked Kilmore.

'I've built up an immunity to the sting of a bee,' said Melly. 'I had a few stings early in my beekeeping days, but once Queen Beth assured her workers that I was a friend they accepted me.'

'How can these wedoubtable bees of yours help us twap the wat?' asked the Colonel.

'We will transfer them to Roddington Hall this afternoon, and you will each be given a role to play in applying The Sting,' he said, a statement that was not greeted with wide-spread enthusiasm.

Only Private Ffuchs-Shafte appeared to welcome the involvement. 'I want to see what I can learn from Queen Beth and her in-flight technique,' she told Nurse Blige, who was fighting the urge to tell Captain Melly to buzz off.

Melly was just preparing a bee-covered comb for transport when Corporal Ready became the unwilling victim of one of his body-shaking fits. He nudged Melly's arm as he went into his 'wey-hey-hey' wail, and suddenly a thousand bees were released and swarming above the heads of the brigade members, who made a mass dash for the truck.

'Stay, Beth, stay,' commanded a perfectly calm and collected Captain Melly.

Queen Beth stayed, and within a minute her worker bees had returned to her side. The crisis was over.

Bernie Biddle was elected to drive the brigade, plus the bees, back to Roddington Hall. Nobody fancied Corporal Biker bouncing them around.

Melly sat in the front passenger seat with the mobile comb-hive between him and Gunner Biddle. He was in a buoyant mood, and felt a real buzz.

Molly Shufflebottom hated the telephone. She could never understand the need for one. Nobody she knew had one of the daft things, apart that is from Lord and Lady Roddington and they would not have wanted her ringing them up. And what could she have said if she had? ''ello, your Ladyship. Molly Shufflebottom 'ere, your kitchen maid what you treats loike a servant. 'ow be you today? 'ow would ma'am like 'er toast this morning?' That's all she'd ever said to her Ladyship in the six years she had worked at Roddington Hall. And about all her Ladyship had ever said to her was, 'Buttered, and make sure the tea is piping hot for a change.'

Molly just could not see the point of being on the telephone if there was nobody she knew who also had one. She could not ring friends, and they could not ring her, so why go to the expense of having one in the house? And the cost! The price of one fourpenny call was as much as she earned in an hour.

She had only ever answered the infernal contraption twice before, the first time when the butler was on his day off. How was she to know which end of the thing to talk into? It was five minutes of twisting and turning and getting tangled in the wire before she heard a voice saying in her ear, 'Put Lady Roddington on this instant.'

'Put her on what?' she had said.

'Just bring her to the telephone immediately,' the voice had commanded in what Molly thought was a very snotty way. Then she had put the receiver back on its rest. How was she to know that this cut off the caller?

Molly remembered that Lady Roddington spoke to her, too, that day. Or rather at her. 'You, whatever your name is, are the dimmest and doziest gal I have ever encountered in my entire life,' she said. Well she obviously had not met her sister, Hyacinth, and how about Harriet next door, who used to put herself out at night instead of the cat?

The second time Molly had answered the telephone was even less successful. It had rung while she was feather dusting it, and because the constant ringing was irritating her and breaking her concentration she had put it in the mop bucket. Still it kept ringing, but with a tinny, echoing noise that was even more annoying. So she picked up the receiver and put her head into the bucket to talk into it.

A voice in her ear said, 'Sorry, I must have the wrong number,' and then she had a strange burring noise in her ear and so she dropped the receiver back into the water. Unfortunately, her head had become trapped in the bucket and her Ladyship was absolutely furious that she had to pay for the blacksmith to come to the Hall to cut her free.

Molly had since quietly taken telephone answering lessons from the village post office operator, Mildred. She was the girlfriend of her brother, Simon, the village policeman and the black sheep of the family, who had reported their Dad just because he poached some pheasant from the Roddington Estate. Didn't stop him eating 'em though, did it?

It just so happened on this Thursday afternoon in April, 1944, Molly was alone by the telephone while the rest of the staff were in the west wing trying to clear up the dreadful mess made by the firemen. She was so startled when it rang that she dropped her tray, which was empty for a change because, luckily, she had been ordered not to carry any more crockery. Molly picked up the receiver and did exactly what she had watched Mildred do.

'Hello, Roddington village post hoffice,' she said, trying to copy Mildred's posh telephone voice. 'How may I help you?'

The voice in her ear said, 'Is that Woddington one-o-four?'

'No, I'm terribly sorry but you have got the wrong number,' she replied, and then put the receiver back on the cradle.

Molly was justifiably proud of her effort. It was the only time she had managed to speak into the right end at the first go. Perhaps the telephone was not such a bad thing after all.

Humming happily to herself, she was just about to head for the kitchen when the telephone rang again.

'Hello, Roddington village post hoffice,' she replied. 'How may I help you?'

'Woddington one-o-four?' a man's high-pitched voice said.

'I've told you once already that this is a wrong number,' Molly said, impersonating how Mildred could sometimes be very cross on the telephone. 'Stop wasting my toime.'

She slammed down the receiver, feeling pretty pleased with herself. Perhaps she could apply for a job as Mildred's assistant. Better pay and better hours than in her present dead end job that was leading her nowhere but to the kitchen.

Molly got a duster and gave the telephone a good clean. It had been used twice in the last two minutes, and she did not want to be accused of wearing it out. She noticed that on the dial it said "Roddington 104". 'Fancy that,' she thought to herself. 'I just wonder if that could be the number of this telephone?'

Her deep thinking was interrupted by the jangling of the telephone again. As she had it in her hands dusting it at the time it was quite understandable that the jolt she got from the sudden bell ringing caused her to drop it. The receiver landed in a large open tin of Mansion House floor polish.

Molly picked it up and held the now extremely sticky receiver to her ear. 'Hello, Roddington village post hoffice,' she replied. 'How may I help you?'

'Surely to goodness this is Woddington one-o-four,'

said the same voice in her ear, now sounding more than somewhat irritated.

Molly looked at the number on the dial. 'No, this is Roddington one-o-four.'

'But that's the number I'm winging, Woddington one-o-four.'

'Sorry, but this is Roddington one-o-four... you probably want the mad house at Woddington,' Molly said, and hung up.

It took her a full minute to get the highly polished receiver unstuck from her ear, and she had just replaced it in the cradle when the blessed thing rang again.

'If you don't stop being a pest I shall call the police,' she said in impersonation of Mildred, who had been bothered by somebody who apparently could only breath heavily into the telephone without being able to talk.

'Please don't weplace the weceiver,' begged the voice in her ear. 'I want to speak to Colonel Waymond Wavenscwoft.'

''e bain't be 'ere,' said Molly, dropping the Mildred voice. ''e be gone to Zumerzet.'

'Oh, dwat it,' said the voice. 'Well, then is Melly there?'

'Speaking,' said Molly, amazed that anybody should ask for her and surprised that her name sounded slightly different on the telephone.

'But I thought you were one of us chaps.'

'Oh no, zur, but oi've got noine brothers.'

'Well listen carefully Melly. This is Field Marshal Montgomewy here.'

Molly looked at the receiver with wide eyes. 'Go along

with you,' she said. 'You'm pulling moi leg.'

'Listen you absolute cwetin, tell Wavenscwoft that Wubble-u-C and the genewals will be awiving at eleven hundwed hours tomowow, Fwiday. Got it?'

'Got what?'

'The message, of course.'

'What message be that, then?'

'That Wubble-u-C, and the genewals, will be awiving at eleven hundwed hours tomowow, Fwiday.'

'You'm already told me that load of old double Dutch. "Rubble, you see," you said, "and the generals will be arroiving at eleven 'undred hours tomorrow, Friday." You don't 'ave to keep saying it. Oi'm not an idiot you know, despite what 'er Ladyship might 'ave told 'ee. Now, what's the message you'm on about?'

'Just wemember what I've told you and pass it on to Wavenscwoft. I can't wing again for secuwity weasons. There's no scwambler on this line.'

'I can do you scrambled eggs if you loike, zur.'

'Melly, I'm warning you, if you mess this up it'll be a court martial.'

'Don't worry, zur. Even oi can't mess up scrambled eggs. Well, not always.'

Monty found he was perspiring more than he did in the desert as he replaced the receiver. He comforted himself that Melly must have been talking gibberish to save himself being understood by anybody listening in. Clever chap.

At Roddington Hall, the eavesdropper was trying desperately to make sense of the telephone conversation he had just overheard. Molly, meanwhile, was buffing

149

the telephone and making it gleam as never before. Amazing what you could do with floor polish. Perhaps she would get one for the Shufflebottom cottage after all. She would save up her next six months' wages.

The army truck, being driven by Gunner Bernie Biddle, with the Brigade and Queen Beth and the honeybees on board, had travelled all of twelve miles in the hour since leaving the Melly farm.

It was another three hours before they came at funereal pace through Woddington high street, where PC Shufflebottom overtook them on his bicycle. He quite understandably thought that there was something suspicious about an army truck going this slowly, and so he waved it down.

He went to the passenger side and put his head through the window, which was a silly thing to do because it had not been wound down. The constable helped clear up the glass and then looked round the truck with a measured eye. 'This be a spot check,' he said.

'I've got two blackheads and a pimple on my bum,' said Sergeant Roper from the back.

'Why were you travelling at only ten miles an hour?' he said to Biddle, fixing him with an officious stare.

'But we've been out for more than an hour,' Biddle replied, which left Shufflebottom temporarily lost for words.

His eye fell on the mobile hive on the front seat.

'Hello, hello, hello, what bee'm we 'ave 'ere, then?'

'Bees,' said Captain Melly.

'Oi can see that with moi own eyes,' said the police

150

constable. 'Oi'm not daft, you know.'

'He's a bloody good actor, then,' said Roper.

'Oi'm a country boy born 'n' bred. and oi knows an 'oive when oi sees one. What bee'm them bees doing in an army truck?'

'They happen to belong to me,' said Melly, doing his best to control his temper that had already been pitched near to breaking point by Biddle's incredibly aggravating driving. He could never ever remember before being overtaken in a moving vehicle by a mother pushing a pram.

'Can you prove it?' asked the constable.

'What d'you mean prove it?' snapped Melly. 'D'you think I carry a bee licence with me?'

'Show 'em Queen Beth's birth certificate,' said Gunner Shorthouse.

Shufflebottom looked to see who was being sarcastic, but could not spot him. Shorthouse was hidden behind the passenger seat.

'This be no joking matter,' warned the constable. 'Stealing bees is a serious offence in these parts.'

'I'm telling you they're mine,' insisted Melly. 'I've just collected them from my farm in Somerset.'

'So you'm going to tell me that you'm a farmer.'

'Of course, I'm a farmer. And a beekeeper.'

'You must take me for being a roight idiot,' said Shufflebottom. 'Oi knows that you'm a captain in the Army.'

'But I am and always have been a farmer,' shouted Melly.

'Arggh,' said Shufflebottom, so you'm impersonating

151

an army officer. That be treasonable, that be.'

Whenever Melly got upset, Queen Beth got upset, too, and she ordered one of her servant bees to work. A drone crawled out of the roof of the hive and made a bee line for Shufflebottom.

The suddenly panic-propelled constable swiped at the bee with a giant hand and missed as it darted on a zig-zag path to his helmet. It got under the rim and started to buzz around inside.

Shufflebottom was doing what looked like the charleston in the middle of the road as the bee continued to circulate inside his helmet.

'All right, Beth,' said Melly calmly. 'Call him off. I think the constable has learned his lesson, and he now knows just who the bees belong to.'

The bee bothering Shufflebottom meekly emerged from the helmet and flew back to the hive.

'Okay, Captain Farmer Melly, you'm can proceed on your way now thank you, zur,' the relieved constable said. He hoped that he had not shown it, but he was petrified of bees. As the truck pulled away, Roper could not resist it. 'You silly b...' he shouted.

Shufflebottom nodded his head. 'It were that,' he said. 'A very silly bee.'

'Any telephone calls for me while we were out?' asked Colonel Ravenscroft as the First WC Brigade sat in the conference room at Roddington Hall waiting for Captain Melly to prepare Queen Beth and her worker bees for battle.

'There were one call from some odd-sounding old

gentleman claiming he were Field Marshal Montgomery,' said Molly, pausing from polishing the floor.

The Colonel instinctively stood up and snapped to attention. 'Good gwief,' he said, 'Did he leave a message?'

'Only that he wanted scrambled eggs,' said Molly.

'Scrambled eggs?' repeated the Colonel, trying desperately to think how he could de-code that message. 'Did he say anything else, Molly?'

'It were a bit of a strange call really,' she said. 'He kept calling me Melly, instead of Molly. Oi wondered if he were getting mixed up with my youngest sister, Millie.'

The Colonel was nearly apoplectic. 'Melly, Molly, Millie! I don't give a damn, you dim, dozy gal,' he yelled. It was the harshest thing he had ever said to anybody in his life, and he was mortified when Molly burst out crying.

'You'm been talking to 'er Ladyship, you 'ave,' she said between sobs. 'Bain't my fault I can't get on with the dratted telephone. It were all that polish on it. Got in moi ears, it did.'

Colonel Ravenscroft was now down on his knees begging forgiveness. 'I'm so sowy, Molly,' he said. 'It was unforgivable what I said to you. Pater always tweated our servants abominably, and I had always sworn not be so wuthless and aggwessive.'

He handed her his khaki handkerchief, still blood stained from when he had held it to his damaged nose. 'Here,' he said, 'wipe your eyes, and then please twy to

153

wemember what else the nice Field Marshal welated to you.'

Molly wiped the tears away, loudly blew her nose and then handed the handkerchief back to the Colonel. 'He kept going on about a message,' she said, trying hard to remember. 'It were zummat to do with eleven generals 'aving just hours to go to a court martial tomorrow.'

'Court martial?' said the Colonel. 'God, did you hear that Sergeant-Major? If we don't get the wat it's going to be a court martial and curtains for me. Pater will murder me.'

'Come, come, Sir,' said Bloomer, embarrassed to see the Colonel on his knees. 'Stiff upper lip, and hall that. We'll get the rat this time, don't you worry. I have great faith in Captain Melly's Queen bee.'

'I hope you're wight, Sergeant-Major,' he said. 'I just wish I had your stwength of mind and wesilience. That comes of being wegular.'

'Quite so, Sir,' said Bloomer, wondering what his bowel movements had to do with anything.

'Oh yes, now oi remembers,' said Molly, as she prepared to return to her floor polishing, ''e also said zummat about some rubble you see, whatever that moight mean. It's going to be delivered tomorrow, with the eleven generals, ready for a big fry day. But oi thinks scrambled eggs are better than fried.'

The Colonel sank back into the armchair, his mind wrestling with thoughts of scrambled eggs, court martials, eleven generals and, now, Wubble-u-C. What frying had to do with it he had no idea whatsoever, unless it had something to do with the breaking of the

154

Enigma code, but that was a complete enigma to him.

'Why, oh why,' he said aloud, didn't I go on that biking holiday to Bavawia? I could now be taking it easy in a German pwisoner of war camp.'

At this point Captain Melly walked in with his bare arms covered in bees. 'Right,' he said, 'I want you all to take a dozen bees to each room and release them into the eyeholes in the portraits.'

There was not exactly a stampede to follow his command. 'Sergeant-Major,' said the Captain, 'give the order.' Bloomer's throat was suddenly constricting, but he knew what was expected of him by his King, Country and WC.

'All right you 'orrible lot,' he roared, making the chandelier above his head shake. 'Get fell in and bung up them eyeholes.'

If they had not witnessed it with their own eyes, none of the First WC Brigade would have begun to believe what happened next. The bees, so accustomed to taking orders, rose as one from Captain Melly's arms and swarmed through every room in the Hall, dropping off a dozen drones at a time to flit through the eye holes in the Roddington family portraits.

Within minutes, a door beneath the portrait of Lord Roddington the Third on the far side of the conference room swung open. Chased out of it by a buzz of bees was a weedy little man with tiny, piggy eyes.

'Your Lordship,' Molly said, giving a bobbed curtsy. 'Oi didn't know you were 'ome.'

The Colonel stared at him. 'Well, Wat,' he said, 'we meet at last. For you the war is over.'

155

Personal memo
from the Prime Minister

To: Field Marshal Montgomery
Thursday, 20 April 1944

Dear Bernie,

So they've caught the Rat! Great news. Let me have every morsel of intelligence that the interrogators squeeze out of him. I want to know what's going on in his mind and, even more important, the mind of his Master, Adolf 'The Housepainter' Hitler. I must congratulate you and the Ratcatchers on a job well done. I have only just received the bare facts, and I look forward to hearing more about just how he was captured when I arrive for tomorrow's crucial conference on Operation Overlord.

You ask about the true identity of Jack the Ripper. I am told that it was one of the old Queen's nephews, who when slashing his victims used to shout, 'Oh, my giddy aunt.' All the breast.

Winston S. Churchill

156

11

IT took six hours of intense interrogation by a dedicated team of First WC Brigade members, working in shifts through the night, before Lord Roddington the Fifth finally cracked and started to make a startling confession.

Colonel Ravenscroft and Captain Melly were the first to try to break him down, hoping to extract any information they could on the plot to assassinate the Prime Minister. They were under orders from Field Marshal Montgomery himself to find out if anybody else was involved.

'You say that you are Lord Woddington, fifth Earl of Wingwood,' said the Colonel, beaming a strong light from his monocle directly into his Lordship's eyes.

'Oh no I do not,' said his Lordship, a thin, rodent-faced man with a stubble of beard and top teeth that protruded over his bottom lip. 'You say that. I say that I am Lord Roddington, fifth Earl of Ringwood.'

'That's what I said,' argued the Colonel. 'You are twisting my words.'

'No, you are twisting your own words,' said his Lordship, who was perfectly calm and collected as he sat cross-legged on the library desk with a glass of milk in his hands and a packet of oatmeal biscuits in front of him.

Captain Melly, playing the good guy to the Colonel's bad guy like he had seen in a Humphrey Bogart film, offered his Lordship a biscuit, which he refused. 'What proof have you got that you are the *real* Lord Roddington,' asked Melly. 'For all we know, you could be an imposter pretending to be his Lordship.'

'May I move over to the wall, please?' he asked courteously.

'Yes,' said the Colonel. 'But no funny twicks. It's no good twying to wun because the place is surwounded with cwackshots from the Wifle Bwigade. They are on every wooftop and behind evewy twee with their guns twained on Woddington Hall.'

'Fat lot of good that will do them when we're here at Roddington Hall,' said his Lordship.

Extremely nimble for a man in his mid-fifties, he leapt off the desk like the great Nijinsky in full flight and bounded to the wall nearest to the French windows. He stood alongside the portrait of Lord Roddington the Third. 'Can you see the likeness?' he asked.

'It's the spitting image of you,' said an impressed Colonel. 'But that's a portwait of Lord Woddington the Third...'

'Roddington,' he corrected.

'You claim to be the Fifth Lord Woddington.'

'R-R-R-R-Roddington,' he said, with an exaggerated roll of the R. He pointed at the portrait. 'That's my grandfather,' he said, bounding back and returning to his cross-legged position on the desk. 'The family always say that I'm his double. If you want to see my own personal portrait we will need to go upstairs to the Blue bedroom.'

Both the Colonel and Melly silently recalled Molly's

story of the throat-slashing in the Blue bedroom, and decided that a visit was unnecessary.

Melly was still not convinced. 'I would not accept an oil painting as proof of your identity,' he said. 'They do wonders with plastic surgery these days. I saw a film recently in which Bette Davis was changed beyond recognition.'

'It was Joan Cwawford,' said the Colonel.

'Always get those two mixed up,' said the Captain. 'but, anyway, the change in her looks was quite astonishing. I would like to see further proof that you are who you say you are. For all we know you could have had facial alterations made by one of Hitler's surgeons. They were leading the way in plastic surgery before this lousy war started.'

'A good point,' said the Colonel. 'That thought had not cwossed my mind.'

His Lordship took a rolled gold fountain pen from the inside pocket of his dust and cobweb covered jacket and wrote on a blank page of a notebook on the desk, 'I am Lord Roddington the Fifth,' and then he signed it with a flourish.

Melly studied the signature. 'That's good enough for me,' he said, passing it to the Colonel.

'Yes, it does have a wather autocwatic style to it,' he nodded. 'I agwee that it is obviously quite authentic. So what made you, one of our twue blue bloods, go over to the other side?'

'It suited me better and was more my style,' said his Lordship. 'And anyway, it was far too cold in the east wing.'

159

Ravenscroft and Melly exchanged meaningful glances. The east wing, clearly the Lordship's reference to eastern Europe where Winston Churchill was already warning of an iron curtain coming down. Just the sort of thing a Nazi would say, because all the Germans were living in fear of the vast and merciless Russian army sweeping their way from the eastern front like an unstoppable red tide.

The Colonel decided it was time to stop pussy footing around. 'Have you at any time been to Germany?' he asked.

'Yes, I was there when the war started,' his Lordship said in a matter-of-fact way.

'Ah, so you admit it,' said the Colonel triumphantly, pleased that his British intelligence service training in interrogating suspects, when he had practised for hours on his mother, had quickly brought results.

'An irresponsible British publishing house brought out a book in the summer of 1939 called *Biking Holidays in Bavaria*,' explained his Lordship. 'I bought a copy and it inspired me to make the trip. I was just starting out on the route from Munich suggested by Hermann Goering when war was declared. I had to cycle home via France during the months of the phoney war.'

The Colonel took that in his stride. 'So you know of Hermann Goewing?'

'I've met him.'

'Met him?' said the Colonel, his monocle starting to steam up with the excitement of it all.

'Yes, he was signing German translations of the book at the Beer Hall in Munich where the Putsch started.'

160

'German copies?' said an incredulous Colonel. 'That was not part of the contract. We did not see a penny in woyalties.'

'It would have been a pfennig,' said Captain Melly.

'A penny, a pfennig, what diffewence,' snarled the Colonel. 'It doesn't change the pwinciple that they were wong to publish a German version without consulting us. I shall take the matter up with our lawyers the minute this wuddy war is over.'

'Who gives you your orders?' asked Melly, deciding to bring the interrogation back on track.

'Who else but Lady Roddington,' he replied.

'Lady Roddington, eh?' said Melly. 'So she's in on this, too. Where is she now?'

His Lordship shrugged. 'Probably the Caribbean or possibly Buenos Aires,' he said. 'She took off with her man, the chauffeur, the minute this whole shebang started.'

The Colonel made a note that she had a German chauffeur called Herman.

'When did she last pass orders to you?' he asked.

'I suppose it was about a year ago,' said his Lordship.

'What were the orders?'

'Get out of my sight,' he said, startling his interrogators by suddenly going into a handstand on the desk.

'That was obviously a code to lie low until you had accomplished your special mission,' mused the Colonel aloud.

'Who would she go to visit in the Caribbean?' asked Melly.

'I think she had an invitation to stay with David in

the Bahamas.'

'David?' said Melly.

'Yes, well he is the Governor out there now.'

'The Governor?'

'Yes, the Governor of the Bahamas.'

'But that's the Duke of Windsor, late the Pwince of Wales, late the King of England,' said Melly.

'That's right, old bean. David,' his Lordship said, now lying stretched out on his back across the desk.

'I'm even more convinced now that we have the wight wat,' the Colonel thought to himself. It had long been rumoured that the man who was briefly Edward VIII before abdicating was a Fascist sympathiser and had close connections with Hitler. Why, there had even been a photograph in *Biking Holidays in Bavaria* of the two of them shaking hands.

He made a note to inform British agents in the West Indies and Argentina to be on the lookout for Lady Roddington, and her chauffeur, Herman the German.

'What's Hitler like?' asked the Colonel, now picking up the pace of the questioning in the hope that he could trap him into a slip of the tongue.

'Quite short, jet black hair parted on the left and with a funny little toothbrush moustache,' he said, adjusting his position on the desk so that he was now sitting upright with his feet in the drawers.

'How well do you know him?'

'How well do I know who?'

'Hitler.'

'Well, I know that he is a former Austrian house-painter whose real name is Schicklbruger, and that he

162

was a corporal during the First World War before launching the Nazi Party, and that while in prison he wrote a book called *Mein Kampf*.'

'Ah, *Mein Kampf*,' said the Colonel, another skeleton rattling in his own cupboard. He had paid ten million marks for the English rights only to find that nobody could decipher Hitler's Gothic-style handwriting. 'You have wed it?'

'I skipped through it,' he said. 'I had some problems with the Gothic style of handwriting.'

'You wed the owiginal German version?'

'But of course.'

'So you admit that you wead German. Do you speak it as well?'

'*Ja, ich spreche Deutsch sehr gut*,' his Lordship said. 'Learned it at my grandmother's knee. The old dear was born and brought up in Berlin.'

As Lord Roddington went through a series of sit-up exercises on the desk, the Colonel took the Captain to one side.

'I've no doubt that we've got our man,' he said. 'The evidence is now overwhelming. Biking holidays in Bavawia with Hermann Goerwing... orders from his wife who has a German chauffeur called Herman... so fwiendly with the dodgy Duke of Windsor that they call him David... a German gwandmother... speaks German fluently ... clearly knows Hitler intimately...'

'I tend to agree with you, but I think we need some firmer evidence,' said Captain Melly, looking in amazement as his Lordship expertly performed a handstand inside the wastepaper basket that he had

163

taken from under the desk.

'Why,' said the Colonel, 'do you think he keeps taking up these extraordinary positions?'

'It's obvious,' said Melly 'He has spent so much time in those narrow corridors behind the walls that he has to keep exercising or risk seizing up. He must have been there for over a year waiting for his chance to get Winston, ever since his spy mistress Lady Roddington ordered him to get out of sight and lay low.'

'But of course. The thought hadn't cwossed my mind. I think we should now let Woper and Biddle loose on him. We've dwained him dwy intellectually and psychologically with our incisive questioning. It will be interwesting to see how he copes with a physical challenge.'

'He's a tough nut to crack,' said Melly. 'Gestapo training, I shouldn't wonder.'

'Woper and Biddle will soon sort him out, west on me.'

'Right you little weasel,' said Sergeant Roper, his fist under his Lordship's nose, 'tell us everything you know about the plot to bump off WC or I'll beat you to a pulp.'

Laughing, his Lordship jumped to his feet on the desktop and started miming as if fencing, his legs bent and his left hand on his hip as he made thrusting motions with his right arm. 'Good show,' he said. 'I like a bit of sport. On guard!'

''ow would you like an early funeral?' said Bernie Biddle, in as menacing a manner as he could muster.

164

'I don't think so, thank you young man,' he said, now sitting in the lotus position. 'I'm allergic to coffin wood. Could kill me.'

Biddle slipped him one of his funeral cards, just in case.

'What do you think if you see somebody walking around like this?' said Roper, doing an imitation of a goose-step march around the library.

His Lordship leapt off the desk, and goose-stepped immediately behind him. 'Great leg stretching exercise, what?' he said. 'Much better than the boring marches of the British soliders.'

He raced back towards the desk, jumping and landing on one foot.

''ow much were you getting paid to knock off Churchill?' said Roper, determined to get straight to the point.

'Well I quite fancied Sarah, but I wouldn't have taken money to knock her orf,' said his Lordship, miffed at the thought that he would even consider it.

'I mean Winston not Sarah Churchill.'

'I have to admit that sort of thing does run in my family, but I've never given the man a second glance. Not my type at all.'

'Are you trying to tell us that you've never plotted against Churchill?'

'Well, now you come to mention it,' said his Lordship, 'I did get very, very angry with him when he crossed the House. It was an extremely disloyal thing to do and I vowed that I would one day get him for it.'

'So you planned an assassination?'

'Sort of,' said his Lordship. 'A character assassination I suppose you would call it. I just wanted to see him ridiculed and exposed for being so self-centred.'

He went into a forward roll and somersaulted off the desk, landing on the floor on the balls of his feet with both arms outstretched.

The sudden movement made both Roper and Biddle jump. 'Oy, no funny games or I'll fill you in,' said Roper, ready to call on his power and skill as a professional middleweight boxer.

Lord Roddington dropped into a boxing pose and shadow-boxed around the library.

'I think we've got as far as we can with him, Sarge,' said Biddle.

'Well we ain't done bad,' Roper said. 'We've got him to confess that he's 'ad it in for WC for a long time and that he vowed to get him.'

'Yeah,' said Biddle, 'and that he was plotting an assassination of sorts, that he wanted to knock off Sarah Churchill and that he likes to goose-step. I would say we've clinched it, Sarge.'

'We have, Bernie boy,' agreed Roper. 'This geezer is The Rat all right.'

In the far corner of the library, his Lordship was standing on his head with his feet against the wall.

It was not until the last pair of interrogators, Private Jennifer Ffuchs-Shafte and Nurse Sheila Blige, started questioning him at six o'clock in the morning that his Lordship finally made a full confession.

His little piggy eyes lit up when Nurse Blige entered

the library, and he performed a series of cartwheels. 'I've had my eye on you all week, you scrumptious little trollop you,' he said.

Nurse Blige instantly came out in goose bumps.

'You can have more than your eye on me, your Lordship,' said Ffuchs-Shafte, 'if you will just answer our questions.'

'Anything you want to ask, you lovely little hussy,' he said, dribble coming down his lips and matting in the stubble on his chin.

'Is it true that you were plotting to assassinate Winston Churchill?'

'What d'you want me to say?'

'Well,' said Ffuchs-Shafte, a puzzled frown on her forehead, 'we just want you to admit that you're The Rat.'

'Right, I admit it. Now can we play doctors and nurses?'

'Just make a full confession, your Lordship,' said Nurse Blige, 'and then we can play whatever game you like.'

'What, even "find the sausage"?' his Lordship said, his piggy eyes as wide as they would ever be.

'I'm game for that,' said Ffuchs-Shafte.

'Right,' said his Lordship, 'let me see now. Where shall I start.'

'Well how you first became involved with that 'orrible 'itler, for instance,' said Nurse Blige.

His Lordship stopped pirouetting around the library, and started to make a sworn statement:

'I Lord Roddington, fifth Earl of Ringwood, do solemnly swear in front of the witnesses here gathered, being Nurse Sheila Blige with the big knockers and

167

Private Ffuchs-Shafte who wants to search for my sausage, that I have been a member of the Nazi Party for just over a year. How's that, my lovely gals?'

'No, you silly man,' said Ffuchs-Shafte. 'We need more than that. You must tell us all about the plot to assassinate Churchill.'

'And then can we play "find the sausage"?'

Ffuchs-Shafte nodded, wondering to herself what an aristocratic sausage would look like.

Lord Roddington continued his statement: 'I have been making notes about the plot to rub out Churchill since the arrival of the First WC Brigade here at Roddington Hall. These notes are to be passed on to my superior, and it is my superior who will decide exactly where and when Winston gets it. While making this confession, I would also like to admit to causing an affray in Piccadilly last Christmas when a lady of the streets ran orf with my wallet. I also confess that it was I who stole the bloomers of the vicar's wife orf her washing line, and it was I who put a frog in the maids' bath in the hope that it would make them come running naked out of the bathroom. One more confession: while at Aintree for the Grand National in 1938 I piddled at the Canal Turn, and I would like ten other fences to be taken into consideration.'

His Lordship spread-eagled himself across the desk. 'That's it you luscious things,' he said, 'now come and find the sausage.'

Ffuchs-Shafte was just about to obey his command when Colonel Ravenscroft and Captain Melly, who had been eavesdropping behind the portrait, came marching together into the room.

'A bwilliant job of intewogation, ladies,' said the Colonel. 'We've now got him bang to wites.'

His Lordship was now under the desk on all fours. 'Come out of there you nasty Nazi,' said Melly. 'It's off to the Tower for you, and we're going to throw away the key.'

It was at this point that the library door swung open, and in walked Dr Hammerskill, the head psychiatrist at Woddington Hall mental asylum.

'Vere iz he?' he asked.

'Where is who?' the Brigade members chorused.

'Mad Lord Roddington, of course,' said the doctor. 'I know zat he is here somevhere.'

His Lordship came crawling out from under the desk and tried to bite the doctor's ankles. 'I have come to take you back, Reichsmarschall.'

'Back?' said the Colonel, his monocle spinning madly. 'Back where?'

'Back to zer asylum, of course,' said Hammerskill. 'You vemember zer nacht zat you broke in und eight patients escaped. Vell Lord Roddington vas the vun who managed to stay on zer vun.'

'Why exactly did you call him Reichsmarschall?' asked Captain Melly.

'Zat is zer name he answers to at zur asylum,' the doctor explained. 'Since coming to us a year ago he has been convinced zat he is vunning the var for zer Germans. Ve are treating him for an extreme case of Hitleritis. Everybody uzed to vant to be Napoleon, but Hitler has since taken over as zer most popular role

169

model for zer nutcases.'

Lord Roddington was now swinging from the chandelier.

'Why exactly does he keep doing all these incwedible exercises? asked the Colonel.

'Zis is vat ve haf taught him to try to cure him,' said the doctor. 'It is my belief zat a fit body leads to a fit mind, and ve haf lots of gymnastics at zer asylum. My theory, based on years of study of the insane, is zat gym vill fix it.'

He signalled for his patient to get up off the floor. 'I vill take him back now, and I apologise for any inconvenience zat I may haf caused,' Hammerskill said. 'I shall be back later on for zer dinner zat is being thrown tonight in honour of Vinston Churchill, but I vill make sure zat der Reichsmarschall stays in zer asylum. He has a naked hatred for Churchill, und must not be allowed anyvhere near him.'

Lord Roddington jumped on to the doctor's back, and he rode him like a horse out to the ambulance waiting in the courtyard.

If they had been in the Battle of Stalingrad, the First WC Brigade could not have felt more shell shocked. 'You wealise what this means, of course,' said the desolate Colonel. 'The Wat is still on the loose. Wubble-u-C will be here five hours from now and we still have not caught the man who is pwogrammed to assassinate him. This could mean a court martial for us all.'

'It could also mean curtains for WC,' said Captain Melly.

'Permission to speak, Sir,' said Temporary Gunner Kilmore.

'Permission gwanted,' said the Colonel wearily.

'There's only one thing for it,' said Kilmore.

'What's that then, Cleverclogs?' asked Sergeant-Major Bloomer. 'Run away and hide, is that what you have in mind?'

'I'll second that,' said Bigger, who had been considering that self same plan all week.

'Quite the opposite, in fact,' said Kilmore. 'We must make ourselves very prominent when the Prime Minister arrives and do our best to confuse the would-be assassin.'

'How do you mean exactly?' asked the Colonel, ready to fall on any idea that just might save him from the ignominy of a court martial and the ridicule of his pater. It reminded him of another of his publishing disasters. He had been in charge of the dust jacket for a book on court martial trials of the First World War. It was called, *The Great Court Cases*. His pater said he would never forgive him when the twenty thousand dust jackets arrived at the publishing house with the forty-eight point heading, *The Great Caught Cases*. It was a mistake anybody could have made.

Kilmore explained his idea in full, and Biddle, Biker, Ready and Shorthouse were detailed to bring the latest consignment of Winstons to the library. There were twelve in all.

Operation Ratcatcher was back in full swing.

TOP SECRET
Read and digest
Personal memo
from the Caravan HQ
of Field Marshal Montgomery
To: The Prime Minister
Fwiday, 21 April 1944

Dear Winnie,

We Opewation Watcatcher

Well, today's the Big Day. Hope you're wearwing your bullet-pwoof overcoat when you arwive at Woddington Hall for the conferwence on Opewation Overlord. It seems the Wat has evaded all efforts to capture him. They thought they had him, but it turned out to be potty Lord Woddington, who has been quite mad ever since that wabied dog bit him in the Balkans. Vewy painful.

The First WC Bwigade will be on wound-the-clock duty to guard and pwotect you, and they have come up with yet another ingenious plan to confuse and, hopefully, capture the Wat. Don't forget to duck old fwiend.

Bernie Montgomerwy

12

PRIME MINISTER Winston Churchill arrived at Roddington Hall in a chauffeur-driven Rolls Royce at 900 hours and again at 915 hours, and again and again at fifteen minute intervals until thirteen WCs had been driven through the gates. Only one of them was the *real* Winston Churchill.

The welcoming army band struck up the National Anthem and 'Land of Hope and Glory' thirteen times, and the ceremonial parade of guards presented arms thirteen times, but only once to the real Winston. It became so bewildering that even the top brass generals, air marshals, commodores and admirals summoned to the meeting became confused as to just who they should be greeting. Field Marshal Montgomery discussed the important issue of forthcoming memoirs with Winston for fifteen minutes before he discovered that he was conversing with a dummy being worked by Gunner Shorthouse.

'Where's the Colonel Wavenscwoft who's in charge of your bwigade, Gunner?' said Montgomery.

'He's briefing the real Prime Minister, Sir,' said Shorthouse, looking up from beneath Winston's elbow.

'Well tell him I want to see him wight away,' said the Field Marshal. 'It's a matter of extweme urgency.'

'Yes, Sir,' said Shorthouse, saluting and then scurrying off with his Winston in tow.

Montgomery looked round the conference room,

finding it disconcerting having a dozen Churchills staring back at him and not one of them the real Prime Minister. One Winston was often too much for Montgomery to stomach. But thirteen! What a great Last Supper they could have together, he mischievously thought to himself.

Colonel Ravenscroft arrived at his side, his monocle glowing red, white and blue with pride following a motivating speech from Churchill who had told him: 'One Churchill is too formidable for most of my foes. With thirteen of us we will rule the world. Never have so few come up with such a devilishly clever plan that will help so many. Congratulations, my man.' The word 'devilishly' had been a real challenge for the Prime Minister's lisp, and the Colonel's monocle had taken the spray.

He delivered his smartest salute to Montgomery. 'Colonel Wavenscroft weporting, Sir,' he said.

'Don't you mean "weporting"?' said Montgomery.

'That's what I said, Sir, with the gweatest wespect. Weporting.'

'Well it doesn't sound like weporting to me. You obviously have twouble with your Rs.'

'You wished to speak to me on a matter of weal urgency, Sir?'

'I did? Oh yes, now I wemember. It's about that Churchill chappie who I thought was Churchill. I discussed some wather discweet matters with him thinking it was the weal Winston. I told him off the wecord that the first volume of my memoirs, *How I Helped Spike Milligan Win the War*, will be published

174

next year pwovided, of course, Opewation Overlord is the success we intend it to be.'

'Yes, Sir,' said the Colonel, trying hard to follow the logic of what was being said to him.

'I just want you to stwess to that Churchill chappie who was not Churchill that what was said to him was top secwet and not to be uttered to a living soul. Do you understand me, Colonel?'

'Perfectly, Sir,' said the Colonel, 'but I can assure you that none of our Winstons will wepeat anything they hear here today.'

'Hear hear,' said Montgomery. 'Now then, where's this Wat fellow we've been hearwing so much about? Have you twacked him down yet?'

'No, Sir, but we think we have got him confused. The weason we have all these Winstons is that it considewably incweases the odds of the Pwime Minister not having the assassin getting a firwing line on him. Our Winstons will circulate thwoughout the full day of this conferwence, and also while the banquet is in pwogress tonight. It is now a good twelve-to-one that WC will survive without the Wat getting a single shot at him.'

The Colonel could sense that something was bothering the Field Marshal, who seemed to be almost sulking.

'Is there anything wong, Sir?'

'What do you mean, wong? Why on earth can't you learn to speak pwoperly.'

'Sir seems to be upset.'

'Of course I'm upset,' said Montgomery. 'Why couldn't

175

you have had a dozen Monties on pawade today as well? My part in this war has been evewy bit as important and as histowically memorwable as Winston's, as will wegister when my memoirs are published.'

'Oh I agwee most pwofoundly, Sir,' said the Colonel, 'but begging the Field Marshal's pardon, we have only had a death thweat against the Pwime Minister.'

'That's not to mean this mad Wat fellow won't take a pot shot at me,' Montgomery said, twisting his beret in rage. 'What a twophy I would make for him. Wommel couldn't get me, and I'm damned if I'm going to let some worthless wat in Woddington do for me. This Desert Wat is too clever and cunning for the Dorset Wat, believe me.'

He put on his beret and adjusted it to its usual jaunty angle. 'This has all become too much of a wat wace for my taste,' he said. 'I'm going home to my cawavan before the wat with the itchy twigger finger twies anything. Tell whichever Winston is Winston that he can discuss my part in Opewation Overlord with me on the blower.'

'Yes, Sir,' said the Colonel, throwing an extravagant salute that nearly removed the eye of the passing Molly Shufflebottom, who dropped a trayful of canapés. 'I will welay your message to the Pwime Minister stwaight away.'

Montgomery returned the salute and prepared to leave. 'One wather personal thing before I go, Colonel,' he said in a barely audible whisper.

'What's that, Sir?'

'D'you think that Nurse Blige would come to my

cawavan with me?'

'I'm afwaid she's tied up with her Winston, Sir. Each member of the Bwigade is in charge of one.'

'Oh, wats,' said Montgomery, and stormed off.

Corporal Ready's Winston was the first one to be shot. He was having a fit by the conference room window at the time, and knocked back the blackout curtains with his elbow. A bullet fired from a high-calibre rifle shattered the window and blew a hole the size of a golf ball between Winston's eyes.

The real Winston looked up from the conference table to see his dummy's head being blown apart. 'For goodness' sake keep that racket down,' he barked. 'We're discussing matters of the utmost importance here. Never have I known so much noise made by so few.'

The odds on Churchill surviving had dropped to eleven-to-one.

Members of the Rifle Brigade posted all around Roddington Hall returned the fire the moment the assassin released his shot from behind a hedge facing the Hall. The only casualty was PC Shufflebottom, who had the top of his helmet peppered with shots as he rode by on his bicycle. He attempted to arrest the entire Rifle Brigade, but finally had to make do with charging his sister, Molly, with being an accessory.

Inside the Hall, the blackout curtains were put back in place and Colonel Ravenscroft called an emergency meeting of all the Winstons. They met in the library, and Sergeant-Major Bloomer held a head count. 'There are twelve Winstons here,' he reported.

'But that just cannot be cowect,' said the Colonel. 'We are down to eleven.'

An embarrassed Corporal Ready made his apologies, and returned the real Winston to the conference room.

'Well, men...'

'And women,' said Nurse Blige.

'...we have awived at the moment of twuth. We now know that the Wat has at long last shown himself. That means we are all now in tewible danger, and must be on our guard evewy single second.'

'Permission to speak, Sir,' said Bigger.

'Permission gwanted, Lance Corporal acting Major.'

'Isn't this a good time to be at least considering opening negotiations with the assassin? We could let him have all the Winstons in exchange for him letting us leave the Hall in one piece.'

'All the Winstons?' said the Colonel. 'You don't weally mean that.'

'Well I suppose we could hold the real one back if we have to, but I think the Rat is too clever to fall for it. He's been out-thinking us ever since we arrived at Roddington Hall.'

'You are a disgwace to our Bwigade with your cowardice,' said the Colonel.

'Does that mean you won't go along with my idea?' asked a disappointed Bigger.

'Well, we'll give it some considewation. But first of all let's see if anybody has got a slightly more positive plan.'

'Permission to speak, Sir,' said Melly.

'Permission gwanted, Captain.'

'I'm wondering if I should perhaps consider sending

Queen Beth and the bees out there to hunt down the killer,' he said.

'That's an incwedibly genewous and unselfish thought,' said the Colonel. 'We know what Queen Beth and the bees mean to you, and you, of course, know the wisks involved. If the assassin gets sight of them he could blow them to smithereens.'

Melly bit his bottom lip. 'I know, Sir,' he said, fighting back the tears. 'But at times like this one has to be prepared to make the supreme sacrifice.'

'Well that settles it,' the Colonel said, his mood suddenly brightening. 'Queen Beth is going to make a bee line for the assassin. How will she know where to find him?'

'Ah, that's where we have just a slight snag,' said Melly. 'Somebody has to volunteer to go out and spread some honey on the assassin's person. It can be on his shoe, his jacket, in his hair. Even on his gun. Anywhere, as long as it is visible to my bees.'

'Permission to speak, Sir,' said Roper.

'Permission gwanted, Sergeant.'

''ow the bleedin' hell can anybody go and smother the assassin in 'oney if one, he don't know what 'e looks like, and two, he don't know where 'e is?'

'Good point, Woper,' said the Colonel. 'I think that wather wecks your plan, Captain.'

'Yes Sir,' said Melly, positively glowing with relief. 'I think it rather has.'

'Permission to speak, Sir.'

The Colonel braced himself when he realised it was Ffuchs-Shafte with her hand up.

'Permission gwanted, Pwivate,' he said, dreading what was coming.

'Why don't Nurse Blige and I wave our knickers out of the window?' she said. 'Then, when the assassin shows himself, our rifle boys can shoot him straight between the eyes.'

'Your bwavewy overwhelms me,' said the Colonel, the blush bouncing off his monocle and bathing Ffuchs-Shafte in a red glow. 'But for all we know this hidden assassin could be what I believe is termed a nancy boy. Hitler's army is full of them, I hear. So you could be wisking all for nothing. But thank you for offering to catch cold for your countwy.'

'Permission to speak, Sir,' said Bloomer.

'Permission gwanted, Sergeant-Major.'

'Why don't we get all the Winstons together and form a circle with them round what is the real WC, like what they do in those cowboy films when the Hindians are hattacking the wagon train, Sir. It halways works for John Wayne, Sir.'

'Good idea, Sergeant-Major. But I fear we would wun too gweat a wisk of the Indians, I mean the assassin, picking the Winstons off one by one.'

'Well how's about detergent tactics then, Sir?'

'I think what the Sergeant-Major means is diversion,' said Tinkle.

'Exactly,' said Bloomer. 'We causes a diversion by 'aving all our Winstons marching around the conference room like what the army band does, criss crossing and going in diagonal and straight lines so that the assassin does not know what Winston is who, Sir.'

180

'Any impwovement on that idea?' asked the Colonel.
The question was greeted with silence.

'Wight then, that's settled. It's marching time.'

Bernie Biddle slowly raised an arm. 'Permission to speak, Sir.'

'Permission gwanted, Gunner.'

'Can we do the funeral march, Sir?'

'Well you can if you wish,' said the Colonel, 'but I think the faster you march the less chance the assassin has of getting you in his sights.'

'Permission to speak, Sir,' said Shorthouse.

'Permission gwanted, whoever and wherever you are.'

'Gunner Shorthouse, Sir,' he said from behind his Winston's shoulder. 'What instrument should I be playing?'

'When?'

'When we're the army band.'

'You don't quite understand, Gunner,' explained the Colonel patiently. 'We're just pwetending to be a band, and marching like them.'

'But I can't march without music, Sir. I keep falling over my feet.'

'Well hang on to Winston,' snapped the Colonel. 'He'll keep you in line.'

Gunner Shorthouse got his way, and the Brigade members marched around the conference room while loudly whistling Colonel Bogey. This did not please the real WC, who at the time was trying to explain to Air Chief Marshal Bomber Harris why he did not think it was a good idea to launch a mass bomb attack on the

181

Isle of Wight as a prelude to the Overlord invasion of Europe.

'The Isle of Wight,' said Winston, shouting to make himself heard above Colonel Bogey, 'happens to belong to us.'

'Ah, of course,' said Harris. 'Silly me. All these islands look the same from twelve o'clock high. I meant to say Jersey. Lots of Krauts there.'

'But we'd be bombing our own people,' said Churchill.

Bomber Harris shrugged. 'Yes, but at least we *would* be bombing,' he said. 'Destroy the morale of the civilian population. That's the quickest way to win a war. It's stupid to adopt a policy of keep bombing military targets. They tend to shoot back, and all that flak coming at you is no fun, I can tell you. We should concentrate on bombing the shyte out of the man...'

'...and woman,' said Nurse Blige.

'...in the street. Bombs away!'

'I repeat,' said Churchill, 'that the civilians on the ground in Jersey are on our side. We want to raise their morale, not destroy it.'

Their little tiff was interrupted by the sound of a speeding bullet shattering glass, and this time Corporal Biker's Winston bought it just as he was doing a military two-step past the window. Wax flew all round the conference room as Winston's head exploded into a hundred pieces.

The odds on WC were now down to ten-to-one, and that was not taking into account the bombs of Bomber Harris.

Again the Rifle Brigade opened up, but they succeeded only in puncturing the wheels of Farmer Woodhouse's tractor.

By the time the conference broke up in readiness for the evening banquet in honour of WC, nine of the Winstons had been shot. Three of them had fallen to stray bullets from the Rifle Brigade.

'But he still hasn't got the weal one,' said a triumphant Colonel Ravenscroft as the conference ended. He was beginning to feel as if their mission to save WC had succeeded, even though the odds were down to three-to-one. It was now night-time, and provided the blackout curtains were kept securely in place, there was, the Colonel considered, little chance of the assassin picking off his target with a long-range shot.

Security was so tight when guests started arriving for the banquet, that the Archbishop of Dorset found himself pinned to the ground and having to explain to an over zealous guard why he was wearing a frock. The lead violinist of the Bournemouth Symphony Orchestra, who were scheduled to give a concert after the dinner, had his priceless Stradivarius smashed to pieces by a rifle butt because the short-sighted sentry thought it was a weapon. The Lord Mayor of Roddington had his chain of office confiscated because it could have been used to try to throttle WC, and the Lady Mayoress was turned away because she was too ugly. 'It's got to be a feller in drag,' said the guard.

When the dinner-jacketed Dr Hammerskill arrived from nearby Woddington Hall he had to sign a document

183

swearing that the mad Lord Roddington had been locked out of harm's way.

'Ve vill not be troubled by him,' he promised. 'Ven I left zer asylum twenty minutes ago he vas doing his exercises vile chained to a vall. All zer ozer patients who zink zey are Hitler haf been locked in zer bunker, and are busy planning how zey can escape to Argentina or, maybe, Manchester.'

The three remaining Winstons, apart from the real one, took it in turns to greet the hundred and twenty guests who arrived for the banquet.

Colonel Ravenscroft and Captain Melly stood either side of the door closely observing every arrival. Nobody was allowed in without their gold-edged invitation ticket. There was only one slight scare when a late arrival tried to get in without a ticket. It turned out that it was the police superintendent who had interviewed the Colonel at PC Shufflebottom's cottage. He was beaten up by two guards when he tried to slip past their cordon after telling them that he was the chief of police. The Colonel came to his rescue. 'That's the Chief of Police,' he shouted. 'Why do you think we're beating him up?' replied the guard.

Ravenscroft breathed a sigh of relief when the final guest had arrived, and the door was bolted and barred. All the windows were blacked out, and members of the Rifle Brigade were on guard each side of every window. All doors were locked, and the secret underground passages in which the mad Lord Roddington had been hiding were deliberately flooded. Even a rat could not have survived.

Each member of the First WC Brigade was on duty in the banqueting hall, dressed as waiters and waitresses. Gunner Biddle nearly blew his cover when he spilt the piping hot soup of the day into the lap of the prima donna of the Bournemouth Opera House. Her piercing scream was observed by the conductor of the symphony orchestra to have been a perfect-pitch high 'c'.

Kilmore and Tinkle busied themselves serving soup at the top table.

'Waiter, what's this fly doing in my soup?' asked the snooty Duchess of Dorset.

'Oooh,' said Tinkle, looking closely, 'looks like the backstroke to me.'

'Waiter, there's a bit of wax floating in my soup,' moaned Rear-Admiral McKavendish.

'Don't worry, sir,' said Roper. 'That came out of Winston's ear when he was shot, so it's in Prime condition.'

Francis Bigger had wangled himself the job of wine waiter, and was managing to drink more than he was serving. Captain Melly guessed he had been imbibing when he overheard him say in a slurred voice to the real Winston Churchill, 'What d'you want, mush, red, white or pink?'

When the Prime Minister, holding a balloon glass of brandy in each hand, waved him away, Bigger said, 'Oh, please yerself. Don't say I didn't offer you any.'

Nurse Blige and Private Ffuchs-Shafte worked alongside Molly Shufflebottom serving the vegetables to go with the medallions of beef that had been prepared by three *cordon bleu* chefs in the vast Roddington Hall kitchen. Molly managed to drop a trayful of roast potatoes on which Nurse Blige slipped. She skidded across the banqueting hall into the lap of the real WC, who, as usual, had a timely quip. He looked down at Nurse Blige's huge cleavage and said, 'Never has the sight of just one pair made one man so happy.'

Private Ffuchs-Shafte arrived with a towel and vigorously rubbed the Prime Minister's trousers. He was enjoying it so much that he decided not to tell her that nothing had been spilled on them. And she was certainly not going to tell him that she knew that anyway.

The banquet was going well, too well for Ravenscroft's peace of mind. He was dressed as the butler, and he had an uneasy feeling that something was wrong. He kept looking nervously at the portraits around the conference room, fearing that he was going to see the mad eyes of Lord Roddington the Fifth peering back at him. He and Captain Melly had personally checked through the invitation list a dozen times and had run security checks on every guest.

'It's going famously, don't you think?' said Captain Melly, who was disguised as a flunkey.

'It's going wather too smoothly,' said the Colonel as he watched Kilmore and Tinkle serving the coffees while Biker, Biddle and Roper helped the waitresses clear the dessert dishes. Shorthouse was standing under the table clearing up the latest debris dropped by Molly Shufflebottom.

'What d'you mean, *too* smoothly?' asked Melly.

'Well it's like one of those tewiffic John Wayne

186

westerns when he's fighting the Indians and he says, "I don't like it. It's too darned quiet out there." Well that's how I feel. I can't help thinking there is something not quite wight.'

Bigger staggered by carrying a huge decanter of port. 'Well he's certainly not quite right,' said Melly. 'I've tried to get him to stay in the kitchen, but he insists that it is his duty to King, country and Churchill to pour the port. Trouble is he's been pouring most of it down his own throat.'

Sergeant-Major Bloomer, dressed as the toastmaster, banged his gavel on the top table. 'My Lords, Ladies and gentlemen,' he roared, making the chandeliers clink, 'pray silence for our distinguished and irreverent guest of honour, the Right Honourable Winston Spencer Churchill.'

Instead of the prayed-for silence, there was a full five minutes of thunderous applause which Churchill drank in like intoxicating wine. 'Thank you for that wonderful welcome,' he said. 'I want to start tonight by paying tribute to a certain bunch of men...'

'And women,' said Nurse Blige, as she refilled his coffee cup.

'...Yes, and as I am so beautifully reminded, women as well, who have risked their lives so that I could attend today's conference and also address you here this evening. Because of a necessary embargo, it will be fifty years or more before their story can be told, but I can tell you that I am deeply in their debt. Just let it suffice to say that they have managed to protect me from a rat who would like to turn our great nation into a sinking

187

ship just like The Titanic...'

It was at this point that Dr Hammerskill jumped to his feet and aimed a pistol at Churchill. And it was at this point that Corporal Ready, standing alongside WC waiting to clear the top table, had one of his fits and involuntarily threw an arm against the Prime Minister, pushing him to one side just as the doctor squeezed the trigger. And it was at this point that the drunken Francis Bigger tripped over the unseen Gunner Shorthouse and crashed into Hammerskill, the port decanter cracking him on the skull.

The misfired bullet parted the hair of Colonel Ravenscroft, who had never been so shocked in his life. 'Goodness gracious,' he said, 'that was a really close run thing.'

He burst out with tears of happiness as he realised that the shock of it all had cured his R-ritis. The Colonel could now roll his Rs with the best of them.

While Kilmore and Tinkle dragged the unconscious Hammerskill away, Churchill continued his speech. 'As I was saying before I was so rudely interrupted, I owe my life to a dedicated brigade of men...'

'....and women,' said Nurse Blige.

'...who are the unsung heroes...and heroines...of this war. I just wish to say that this is their finest hour. Please join with me in a toast to the First and Last WC Brigade.'

Under fierce interrogation by Colonel Ravenscroft and Captain Melly, Hammerskill admitted that he was a German agent whose real name was Friedrich von

Hammersküll. He had been sent to England a year earlier with the mission to kill Churchill. He had indoctrinated the mad Lord Roddington into believing he was a German Reichsmarschall and allowed him to escape because he knew he would cause a diversion and take the spotlight off himself.

'I cannot believe zat I haf shot down zo many Vinstons, yet he is still making his damned speeches,' he said. 'Never has vun man been a pain in zer arse to zo many.'

Later that night, as they were being honourably discharged, Colonel Ravenscroft asked each of the brigade what they would do now that, for them, the war was over. They answered in turn, as they shook the Colonel's hand.

Bernie Biddle: 'I'm going to go home and start burying people again. That will make me really happy.'

Johnny Biker: 'I'm going to go back to being a wall-of-death rider, then I might try that acting lark. I want to find a street paved with gold.'

Sydney Roper: 'Yeah, and man'll land on the moon. I shall carry on boxing for a few more years, and then go into pictures. I fancy meself up on that big screen.'

Jack Ready: 'No idea what I will do, but I'll fit in somehow, wey hey hey.'

Stanley Shorthouse: 'I'm going to become a jockey and win all my races by a short head.'

Kenneth Tinkle: 'Oooh, I dunno. I'll muck about for a while and then I think I might become a doctor and see if I can't tap a few funny bones.'

James Kilmore: 'Like Kenneth, I'm going to concentrate on a medical career and maybe I'll be able

189

to carry on with a nurse or three.'

Francis Bigger: 'Ooh, well, uh, um, ah... what can I say? You'll be a-m-a-z-e-d at what I'm going to get up to. Yes, missus, amazed. I think I'll go up Pompeii and start from there.'

Tiger Bloomer: 'To be honest, Sir, I thinks I'll sign on for another few years in the Harmy. It's the only life what I knows, and I would find it ain't 'arf cold, mum, if I were out of uniform.'

Jennifer Ffuchs-Shafte: 'Well my stars say I'm going to marry somebody with a mansion in Suffolk and who wears a monocle. So I'll just have to see if I can bump into him one fine night.'

Sheila Blige: 'It's going to be a nurse's life for me, darling. Probably in the East End where I comes from. Bedpans, enemas and all that carry on. What a giggle it's going to be, eh?'

Simon Melly: 'I can't wait to get back to my farm and my beef, bees and beer. My Jersey cows and Good Queen Beth will see to it that I have a future filled with milk and honey, provided the cows stay sane, of course. And what about you, Sir?'

Raymond Ravenscroft: 'Well I'll look for somebody to settle down with me at my country home in Suffolk, and I don't think I'll have to look far. Then I shall take over Pater's publishing company, and in fifty or so years time I shall publish the true story of Operation Ratcatcher.'

'And what will you call it?' asked the Captain.

'Cawy on England,' said the Colonel.

Personal memo
from the Prime Minister

To: Field Marshal Montgomery
Saturday, 22 April 1944

Dear Bernie,

So all's well that ends well. Thoroughly enjoyed last night's bash, and I'm sorry that you missed it because you were sulking in your caravan. The First WC Brigade did their duty to a man (and woman). I am going to see to it that Colonel Ravenscroft is rewarded with promotion to Lieutenant-General, that's provided he keeps a promise to publish my memoirs. We have decided on a title: The Churchill Dairies. That's what it says on the dummy jacket he has sent me, but I would have thought Diaries might have been more commercial. Please destroy this letter. The original will help keep my family from future destitution. Carry on, England.

Winston S. Churchill

DON'T MISS THE OTHER HILARIOUS TITLES IN THIS **CARRY ON** SERIES

And don't forget that all the *Carry On* classics are also available on the Cinema Club video label, and distributed by VCI, price £4.99 each. Watch the videos, read the books... and *Carry On laughing*.